David Freeman grew up in Plymouth, and spent much time in Cornwall. He is married to Rosie, and has three grown-up children and 11 grandchildren. He enjoys writing stories for them. He was a teacher and has travelled widely, making many friends and helping the disadvantaged by setting up schools and training teachers. He has authored several books on education. *Rame* is his first novel.

Dedicated to:

The true Cornish people who overcame poverty and troubles to survive and thrive.

David Freeman

RAME

AUSTIN MACAULEY PUBLISHERS™
LONDON • CAMBRIDGE • NEW YORK • SHARJAH

Copyright © David Freeman 2022

The right of David Freeman to be identified as author of this work has been asserted by the author in accordance with sections 77 and 78 of the Copyright, Designs and Patents Act 1988.

All rights reserved. No part of this publication may be reproduced, stored in a retrieval system, or transmitted in any form or by any means, electronic, mechanical, photocopying, recording, or otherwise, without the prior permission of the publishers.

Any person who commits any unauthorised act in relation to this publication may be liable to criminal prosecution and civil claims for damages.

This is a work of fiction. Names, characters, businesses, places, events, locales, and incidents are either the products of the author's imagination or used in a fictitious manner. Any resemblance to actual persons, living or dead, or actual events is purely coincidental.

A CIP catalogue record for this title is available from the British Library.

ISBN 9781398484344 (Paperback)
ISBN 9781398484351 (ePub e-book)

www.austinmacauley.com

First Published 2022
Austin Macauley Publishers Ltd®
1 Canada Square
Canary Wharf
London
E14 5AA

Many thanks to my wife, Rosie, and family who read and checked this novel.

Cover photo by Derrington Locksmith

Chapter 1
A National Triumph and a Personal Tragedy

"The sea has neither meaning nor pity." [1]

The impact of the water shocked the breath out of his body. The unseen hand forced him down, down into the swirling ocean. Filled with desperate panic, Dominic struggled to free himself, but the iron grip on him was relentless; his neck was in a vice. He twisted and turned. His lungs were bursting. *I'm drowning...* the thought pounded in his head. The murky green water grew darker.

"Aagh!" he screamed and awoke sweating, entangled in the bed sheets; his heart still pounding. Relief swamped him as he realised it was the nightmare again; the recurring horror that so often terrorised his nights.

Prue, hair all tousled, rushed into his room in her long nightgown. "Dom, dear, are you alright?"

He reassured her. "It's my old nightmare again."

"Shall I tell Dad?"

---

[1] Anton Chekov

"No. No way," he panted, "he would never understand. He'll only tell me to stop being a cry baby."

His sister set down her candle. "Here, you have this one till you're calmed down."

"Thanks Prue." He settled back on the pillow with a sigh, as she went out. *Why? Why does this keep happening?* He wondered, as his heartbeat settled. It had begun when he was seven. For years it had struck fear into him when he least expected it. There seemed no rhyme or reason to it. He had loved the sea and swimming in it as long as he could remember. He lay pondering and watching the first grey of dawn lightening the sky.

For as long as Dom could remember, Prue had been like a young mother figure to him. Even when she was only seven and he was three, she had cared for him. He had been a timid boy and she had always soothed his fears.

Dom, Dominic in full, received his name from the place of his birth: the village of St Dominick, which nestled high above the River Tamar, under the lee of Kitt Hill. His parents, Ned and Mattie Martyn, had travelled the twelve miles up from their home in the seaside village of Kingsand, so that Mattie could have the reassurance of her mother for the birth. All had been to no avail. The labour was long and painful; the baby was breech and his mother had lost so much blood that she passed away before the doctor, who came from nearby Callington town five miles away, could get there. Grief and sadness had filled the house. Young Prue was bewildered. Where had her mother gone? The consolation for her was a new baby brother to adore and care for. Ned had never recovered. The grief at losing the love of his life had filled him with bitterness and caused him to cast the blame on his new-born son as the cause of the tragedy. No amount of words from the older grieving parents could change his mind.

Little Dom, as he grew into a sensitive lad, felt the atmosphere of heaviness always around his father, who never seemed to want to touch him, let alone play with him. Once Dom had overheard his father, in frustration at the lack of a mother for his son, saying bitterly to Prue, "If it wasn't for that boy, your mother would be here now."

Uncomprehendingly, Dom felt a cloud surround him with blame. So... it was his fault!

Later on that night, as Prue had said a prayer with him, he asked, "Prue, is it really my fault that Ma died?"

She glanced at his pinched and anxious face and quickly cuddled him. "No, no Dommy! It was not your fault. How could it be? You was only a baby."

He was slightly reassured but the revelation dogged him, especially as Ned never had a word of encouragement or affection for him. He seemed to be always finding fault and Dom became the butt of negative comments. He got in the way... he was no help... he was a skinny runt... it was time he stopped being a cry baby.

Their home was a little cottage in Back Street, Kingsand, just twenty yards from the sea. They rented it from Mr Jones who lived in Plymouth. He had inherited it from an aged relative. Apart from claiming his rent each week, Tobias Jones was mostly an absentee landlord and a disagreeable one at that. He was generally unwilling to spend any money on repairs to the property, unless it was absolutely necessary. Typically, Ned hated him for the power he had over him and Tobias returned the feeling, only tolerating him if he paid the rent. Back Street was really not a street but a steep, muddy lane with many potholes and troughs which filled up in the rains and blew dust in the summer. If you walked a few hundred yards down, the lane narrowed so much you could almost touch both sides at once. Next you came around the sharp elbow-bend of the lane which protected dwellings from harsh sea winds; suddenly, the sea air and the full view of the bay hit you. The view was stunning, enabling you to see right across Plymouth Sound, the deep bay frequented by many boats heading for Devonport docks in Plymouth. On a sunny summer's day, you might think you were in a foreign, tropical land; it was so beautiful. Emerging from the lane, you were standing on The Cleave, the only sea wall boundary to keep the unpredictable sea back from the line of cottages facing the ocean in all weathers. It could be a precarious, even a dangerous, place in a storm.

Kingsand was named after the visit, in a past century, when Henry, the earl of Richmond, visited them at the end of the Wars of the Roses. Henry was plotting to overthrow Richard III and was supported by Richard Edgecumbe, the earl from the nearby Mount Edgecumbe estate, which bordered the village. It was a hasty meeting as The King's men had been alerted and were coming from Plymouth to seize him. Henry was warned and fled back to his ship. In 1485 Henry would become Henry VII. The story left its mark, as the pub he visited was renamed 'The King's Arms' and the lane which he had used, coming up from the beach, was henceforth grandly named 'The King's Way'.

This royal event had elevated the pride of the village and had put neighbouring Cawsand's nose out of joint. Ever since, down the years, the rivalry was bitter between the two villages. It was further exasperated by the fact that, in

Cawsand, there was a smuggling ring, which brought unwanted attention from authorities to both villages. The villages clung to the hillside; their dwellings huddled together, clinging tenaciously above the sea like limpets on a rock; a hotchpotch of small cottages. They were protected to some extent from the wild sea winds by the peninsula reaching to Penlee Point. Yet they were always held in thrall to the ocean: their bullying enemy, which wrestled them in the winter, hurling its waves at them like water cannons. In the summer it was their smiling, shimmering, beguiling friend. Always, throughout the year, it was their livelihood.

From above, the two villages appeared to visiting 'furriners' to be one community, as they nestled in the fold of hills under Maker Heights. But the deep rivalry and suspicion divided them on several issues; not only the distant visit of the king. As a result of a quirk of ancient history, one village was in the foreign shire of Devon and the other, officially located in trusty Cornwall! In Saxon times the land of Maker Parish, directly above Kingsand, had been given to a distant bishop and later transferred to the King of Wessex. So now Kingsand was Devon county: "Dem'n" as the locals called it. Cawsand (Cawsun) derived from 'Cows on the sand' was in Cornwall. The boundary line ran down the coomb – a valley – and was indicated by a stone marker on the wall of the nearby house. It crossed Garrett Street, the long street joining the two villages. With one step you could move from one county to the other!

Set in the sheltered crook of the arm of land leading to Penlee Point, this was, later still, to become known as Cornwall's forgotten corner. In the 1800s this could well have described most of Cornwall. The Cornish peninsula, the far south west of England, has, throughout history, been detached, remote and slightly wild. The two villages' beautiful but remote setting reflected the isolation of Cornwall. It bred that independent spirit of the Cornish. Throughout history this whole south-west peninsula of England, inhabited by the ancient Celtic Dunmoni and Cornovii tribes, in Devon and Cornwall, remained untouched by Roman or Saxon rule. It was too remote, too wild and without value. Originally, before the Romans, Phoenician traders from Spain and Portugal had been attracted to trade for the rich copper and tin in the far south west. Still today, many typical Cornish reflect those forbears; they are dark-haired and relatively smaller but wiry in physique and stature.

Over the centuries, Cornwall grew its reputation for an independent spirit, keeping its own language, derived from the Celts. The Cornish were distrustful of government and 'them up London' who could not possibly understand, and generally did not care, about their deprivation and way of life as men of the sea. So far from any main highway route, in the 1800s the two villages only claim to fame was the pilchard trade and its link to Plymouth's markets. The main route was by boat across Plymouth bay, around the Edgecumbe headland. The alternative was that, by poor roads, you could make your way over the natural divide of the River Tamar by way of a small ferry at Cremyll, but it took time. Originally, this was a rowing boat in the eleventh century; it was now in the 1800s, under the control of the wealthier Edgecumbe family.

It had been the year 1805 when Dom was born. As the little forlorn family, grieving their loss, made their sad way back into Kingsand village, the streets were rejoicing at the news of the battle of Trafalgar and Nelson's victory over the combined Spanish and French fleets. The wild joy conflicted against their mournful hearts, paining them. As they passed 'The Rising Sun' pub, up by the small green at the top of their lane, men and women, dancing jigs and wild with drink, shouted out to Ned.

"Hey Ned, we beat them old Frenchies and them Spanish dogs – good ole Nelson!" Nelson was a favourite hero in the area for he and his lover, Lady Hamilton, had once spent the night at The Ship Inn, just a few hundred yards away over the boundary line in rival Cawsand. Any news from Plymouth came piecemeal and much delayed. These revellers had not yet heard that Nelson had died in the great battle. The crowd's wild rejoicing jarred cruelly against Ned, who shunned them all, filled only with grief and worry about how he would live without his Mattie.

Old Maudie met them next door to their little cottage. A shrunken woman, looking older than her forty years, her deeply lined face, like an ancient map, showed her hard life. She always wore a shawl wrapped around her skinny frame. Her teeth were yellow and stained but she had a heart of gold. Her gangly son Sol, aged 18 was sheltering behind her, despite being nearly six foot tall. There had never been any sign of a father. Sol tentatively put his bony hand on Prue's shoulder and patted her wordlessly in sympathy. Maudie took the baby in one arm and hugged Prue with the other.

"I be so, so sorry at yer loss," she muttered to Ned. "'Tis a sad, sad thing; poor Mattie." She shook her head sorrowfully. "But 'tis good yer work's been kep' for you by good ole young Sam Pethick," she added.

He nodded and pushed past to their door. This was something. Big Sam was his boss in the pilchard fishing trade and Ned was a hard worker. At least they wouldn't starve.

Chapter 2
Friendship of Rivals

"We are like islands in the sea, separate on the surface but connected in the deep." [2]

Dom grew up there in Back Street, which was the poorer area of Kingsand. He was lanky and skinny; his face sunken, he was unable to shake off brooding fear and blame, always beneath the surface – and the dreams didn't help. Prue tried to bolster his confidence. He was "a good-looking boy", she told him. She said he had his father's prominent nose, but not his dark eyes. "You have Ma's eyes," she told him, "cornflower blue they are, like a summer sea – and her wavy brown hair."

Prue and he used to go everywhere together while he was younger. One occasion he never forgot. They were visiting a relative who had the misfortune to live in Cawsand. As they ventured one morning over the 'boundary' into Garrett Street, they hadn't gone far when a harsh, sneering voice cut into them like a knife.

---

[2] William James

"What you doin' 'ere? Snobby scum from Kingsand!" Prue's protective arm held seven-year-old Dom's shoulder fast.

They turned to see the flashing black eyes under an unruly thatch of dark, spiky hair; the full lips curled in mockery. Dom shrunk onto Prue's dress.

Prue answered bravely back, "We're visiting our aunt – leave us alone!" She walked on.

The voice snaked through the air after them: "Hoity-toity – stuck up snob – jest you wait!"

They walked on.

"Wh-who was that?" faltered Dom in a shaky voice. His heart was skipping a beat, fear flared up in him, his knees were shaking.

"That's Rydd, Bruiser's son – good riddance!" she replied.

"Who's Bruiser?"

"Bruiser is Bill Bolitho. He's a nasty man."

Dom only hoped they wouldn't meet him. They reached the high end of the street which Dom loved to call his look-out. Prue hoisted him up to look down over the wall to the curving beach with many fishing boats 60 feet below. He gazed out to Penlee woods opposite, out to the sea beyond.

"I like it 'ere," he said.

"Well you may," said Prue grimly, "but we don't have many friends outside Kingsand. Come on, let's find Aunt Lettie; she'll have some currant buns."

Now, aged 13, as he lay, recovering yet again from this nightmare, he continued to think. He was a few months short of being 14 years old. For years the drowning nightmare had dogged him. *Why? And why was there a force, like strong hands, holding him down?* As dawn broke grey over the rooves opposite and the Spring sun was reflected in their windows, Dom decided to get down to Girt Beach to wash away his sweat and re-encounter the sea he knew and loved.

As he slipped out of the house and down the crooked lane, he could hear the ever-present rhythmic 'shushing' of the waves breaking on the beach. He emerged on the Cleave and it caused him to blink as the rising sun was blazing from over Jennycliffe on the other side of Plymouth Sound. The water was so different from that scary, stormy sea of his dream. It was jade-green to be sure, but smooth as a glass mirror as it unfolded in gentle waves on to the shingle.

The beach was deserted, except for old Sam Pethick, grandpa to Davy, always up early, who was standing by the railings outside the London Inn, mending some nets for his son. Sailor Sam, as they called him, was a gnarled old seasalt. He waved a greeting to Dom as he sucked on his pipe. Sam was always ready to tell his sea tales. He had once been press-ganged into the navy as a young man and had served for many years until he was too old.

Girt Beach, Sailor Sam had once told him, in answer to his question, was so named after the practice of tying up the fishing boats, fore and aft, to prevent them being broached sideways and damaged by the incoming tide. They were then 'girt'. This morning none of the boats were girt; most were out early to get the best catch of pilchards. Ned was with them along with his boss, Davy's dad, sometimes called Young Sam. *Perhaps,* thought Dom, *his friend Davy would join him this morning, as he lived at the end of the Cleave right by the beach.*

Dom plunged gingerly in. As always, the fresh cold water took his breath away but, in no time, he was swimming fast and the water soon seemed warmer to his body as it washed away the effect of his dream. The morning sun had created a dazzling path of light ahead of him and he broke joyously into it.

"Hey, Dom!" Came a call from the Pethick's cottage, as Dom's friend had spotted him. He was throwing off his clothes and stood there, a stocky, well-rounded figure (for Davy loved his food). He was of typical Cornish stock, always tanned despite the early season, thick dark hair and dark eyes. Sturdy and compact, Davy was built for work, which was just as well as his father intended to work him hard in his fishing business. He had few words but was steady and as dependable as a rock. He dove in off the wall to join Dom and popped up beside Dom with his dark curls dripping. The two had been fast friends since as long as they could remember, because Davy's dad, Sam Pethick, had been Ned's boss in the pilchard business for several years, and so there was a lot of sharing. They splashed one another in the warm summer sunshine and swam out, chattering away.

"Shall we go and look up Tris?" asked Dom and Davy nodded, turning to do his fast crawl towards Tristan's home.

Tristan lived on the Cawsand side halfway along Garrett Street. He was the son of Pastor Kenny and lived at the small Manse adjoining the relatively new Congregational church. Pastor Kenny and his church were still viewed with suspicion by many of the villagers as it had only been built just over twenty years ago in 1793. It had originally been called a Meeting House for those who broke away from the Church of England since the seventeenth century and became known as

Dissenters or Separatists. This seemed suspicious to many of the villagers and, in any case, twenty years was a very short time for the Cornish to accept a new way of anything, especially church. Traditional Anglicans worshipped either at the very old St Germanus church near Rame or, if they were wealthier and could manage to ride up the steep hill, at Maker Parish Church up on the Heights. Chapel folk, who were themselves originally Dissenters, kept to themselves in Kingsand, worshipping just a short way up from Dom's house. They were suspicious of such a group in the rival village. Similar suspicions and antagonism were shared by the traditional Anglicans who regarded themselves as the true Christians and could not countenance anyone breaking away from the traditional parish church.

Dom, like his dad and many of his neighbours, was never sure about Pastor Kenny, particularly as Ned never had a good word to say about any church, blaming God for the loss of his Mattie. Dom, too, could not understand why his Ma had to die and leave them all forever.

Tris and Dom had met while Dom was out swimming, when a young pup belonging to Tris had fallen from the rocks into the sea which had a swell that day. Every time that Tris, who was fully clothed, tried to reach his dog, the little chap was thrust against the rocks and carried out again by the wave. When Dom, who had been swimming further out, saw the problem, he had shouted, "I'll get him!" Using the crawl stroke, Dom quickly made his way to the little pup and saved him. He carried him back to Tris on the rocks. Tris introduced himself and his ready smile and gratitude warmed Dom. The lad was good-looking with an open face, blond hair and had honest bright blue eyes. Tris talked a bit posher but they became fast friends, especially bonded by the loss of a mother; Tris' mum had died of diphtheria a couple of years ago. Dom soon admired Tris' athleticism and strong physique, compared to his own skinny body. When they swam or played games, Tris could easily beat him but never gloated; and sometimes, Dom suspected, he allowed him to win. He was easy in friendship and good with words. He soon won over Davy, who overcame the worry about Tris coming from 'the other side'. They decided it was best for the time being to keep their friendship to themselves.

On this bright day, "Let's go to Rame for the day, we can be free there," urged Dom, "and anyway, Prue has been threatening that school will start for me soon."

She had said with forced brightness, "You're going to start school. Mrs Trevelyan's starting one. You'll like that!"

He had been shocked.

"It's very kind and generous of her," she continued, "she said she wants to help children to gain knowledge."

"Bother her and bother knowledge!" said Dom moodily. "Why can't she mind her own business?"

The last thing he wanted was to be indoors every day but it seemed there was no way out. Ned had seen to that; he had changed his mind about 'edecation', as it was free and it would get Dom out from under his feet.

"I have to go too," said Davy sullenly, when the boys next met. They felt life was closing in on them.

Tris smiled and was more positive. "My dad says it will be good for us and broaden our minds."

"Huh," replied Davy, "I don't want no one messin' with my mind."

Neither he nor Dom relished the thought. The only schooling Dom and Davy had was a few attempts by Prue at getting them to read and count. Ned had never really valued 'edecation'.

"Mmm," said Davy begrudgingly, "but what about kids from both Cawsand and Kingsand havin' to attend the same school? There'll be trouble."

"My dad says this rivalry *will* end in trouble," explained Tris one day. "Perhaps this'll help us live together better. Dad says we're all meant to care about everyone equally."

This sounded good to Dom, *but was it ever possible?*

He smiled, "You always see the good side, Tris. Maybe it'll do us some good. Come on," he said, "let's go. Our dads are out on the boats, will your dad mind?" he asked Tristan.

"No, he's gone to visit the sick in Port Wrinkle," said Tris, "So we're good to go!"

The plan was to smuggle some bread and fish out of their homes and meet up at Penlee Point, the promontory at the far end of Penlee woods which cloaked the cliff on the far side of Cawsand. Dom and Davy skirted around by the high road to avoid trouble in Cawsand.

At Penlee the three lads followed the undulating rough cliff path around the wild, rocky bay with no one in sight. The open sea lay before them, glinting blue and silver. Rame Head loomed in front of them, looking like the head of a great reptile crouching out with its back on the mainland and its nose pointing into the sea. *It would be a great day,* thought Dom; the sun was unusually warm in the Spring sky.

It was Simple Sol who had first pointed it out one autumn some time ago, after they had explored the steep lane at the back of Kingsand, picking blackberries. They had emerged on the top of Maker Heights and had been rewarded by the stunning view, on the one side, of Plymouth and Devonport docks with several large schooners there, a passenger steamer and other small boats clustering around them. Wild Dartmoor lay behind Plymouth town, it's green and purple hills rising up to Hessary Tor in the far distance. Dom had heard that the famous Dartmoor prison was behind it, housing French prisoners of war. Turning to the other side, in front of them, was the stunning view of Plymouth Sound bay stretching out to the distant sea horizon. About a mile or so out from where the lads stood, there was activity which caught Dom's eye. Several boats and a bigger ship were working on a wall.

"Whatever are they doing?" he asked Sol.

"They be b-building a wall to stop the big waves swampin' Plymouth," replied Sol, "Ole Sam told me." He struggled for a moment to stutter, "S-Sam says it's a br-br-breakwater."

"Who'd a thought you could build such a wall in deep sea?" Dom said in amazement.

As they turned further to the far right, there for the first time, Dom had seen Rame Head and its wildness had tugged at his heart.

"I've got to go there!" He had breathed in excitement.

On their return down to Kingsand, Sol wanted to go swimming. Despite his problems in relating to people and expressing himself, when he was in the sea, he was a different person; he swam like a fish. Watching him dive in off the rocks with complete confidence. Dom shook his head in amazement. He then decided, that soon, he would take the first opportunity and go and explore Rame on his own. He had a feeling it was going to be a special place. He didn't know the cliff path route at first, as Sol told him the best way would be on the road towards Whitsands, up to St Germanus' church.

Next day, a few hundred yards past the old church, he emerged on a high hill with the ram's head stretching out ahead of him topped by its tiny hut, like a horn on its head, which was, he later discovered, St Michael's chapel and which had been there since the 1300s. With mounting excitement, he had hurried down the long steep hill to the narrow neck of rock which still joined Ram's head to the mainland. He stepped on to the narrow path across the rocks cautiously, affected by the rough waves pounding on jagged rocks either side of him, a hundred feet below. Dom gasped with delight at the wildness of it as the wind gusted across the gap. It buffeted him hard, almost as though some force was resisting his advancement on to the headland. The gulls added to the atmosphere by screaming like demons and wheeling wildly around and below him. To fall from that precarious bridge of land, he realised, would be a gruesome end on those razor-sharp rocks. He won his way across and climbed the steep hill up some rough footholds, worn in the turf over the years; it was punctuated by rough rocks to clamber over.

Arriving at the little stone-built shelter at the top, which seemed like the ruin of a miniature church, he caught his breath and enjoyed the panoramic view on all three sides. To the left was Penlee Point with his familiar village home hidden out of sight behind it. In front of him was nothing except the ocean and the wide horizon. Out there was a single schooner with sails billowing as it headed out to sea, leaving a trail of foam behind it. Over there, somewhere, was France, their long-time enemy. He had heard the men speak about the port of Roskoff which they sometimes traded with. Before he was born, in the days of the French Revolution, there had been huge fears of French pirates, and, later, of an invasion by 'Boney', Napoleon Bonaparte. At the thought of that name Dom shivered. As a young boy Ned had threatened him in anger when he had broken something or crossed him, saying, "Boney will get you one night. He captures stupid boys."

This had added to his fears and often kept him awake.

Turning away from his childhood memories, he gazed to his right and saw Whitsands Bay curving miles into the distance. The beach of tawny golden sands was miles long; it was low tide. It looked very appealing but Dom had heard stories of the treacherous undertow caused by the outgoing tide. Last summer there had been two boys from Port Wrinkle who had drowned, as the strange currents dragged them under. There had been shipwrecks too, in wild storms, for the rocks around the headland were hidden, like shark fins, under the waves.

But it was the distant horizon, as straight as a ruler, dividing turquoise sea from a pale blue sky, that compelled Dom's gaze. It gave him a sense of wide, open freedom and space. Here his spirits were lifted out of his cramped home with its tensions. Here he could dream without limits. He stretched out contentedly on the scrubby grass outside the chapel, dreaming of being an explorer and sailing far beyond. *This,* he decided, *would be his retreat; his escape; his secret place.* Here he could be himself with no one to bother him.

There was a sense of peace in the tiny rough chapel with its rough granite and slate walls and its window spaces open to the wind. He wondered who had prayed here in years past?

Since that first day months before, he had shared it with his two trusted companions, letting them in on his secret "on pain of death," he had warned in mock seriousness, but they got the point.

Now, trying to put out of their minds the looming thought of school, they took the low cliff path from Penlee Point, which Dom had discovered. It was rough and meandered up and down, but was quicker than going around by road. At Rame they first scaled the cliff side and gathered seagull's eggs, despite the screaming gulls whirling around them. Next, they climbed up on to the narrow neck of land to begin the ascent to the top. Dom was full of enthusiasm. To his surprise, as they stepped on to it, Tris looked bothered.

"Whatever's wrong with you?" asked Dom.

Davy turned to see.

"It's nothing." He shook himself.

Dom and Davy began wondering what this place was about and how long it had been here. Tris began to answer their questions, because, knowing he was going to visit, he had asked his dad to tell him about it. The old Cornishmen knew Rame Head as 'Pen den Har'; it meant a fortified headland. Its present name, he had said, meant a ram's head.

He told them it was a watching place, around the time of the Spanish Armada and, having spotted the fleet, a beacon had been lit to warn the country of the pending invasion. This had alerted Francis Drake on Plymouth Hoe, where he was playing his game of bowls. He had been so sure of himself that he insisted on finishing his game before joining his navy.

"Wow!" said Dom as Tris finished. "That's exciting! I wish I had someone like your dad to teach me history."

"Francis Drake sailed right around the world and returned to Plymouth, where the Queen knighted him and made him Sir Francis Drake," added Tris.

This fascinated Dom and awoke in him a desire to learn history; to travel and to have adventures.

After they had eaten their bread and fish, throwing crumbs for the birds, Tris suddenly said, "Let's go now."

"What?" exclaimed Dom in surprise.

"Why?" asked Davy, equally surprised. "We've only been here a short while."

Tris looked uncomfortable. "I just get a funny feeling here – I don't like it. There's a feeling of foreboding."

"What's 'forebodin'' mean?" asked Davy.

"It's just a feeling of something wrong about to happen – something dangerous." Tristan shook himself again.

"You're imagining things Tris," said Dom reassuringly. "What could go wrong in this beautiful place?"

"I hope I'm wrong," he replied, looking unconvinced.

Reluctantly, as the best of the day was over, they made their way back down.

None of them had seen the dark figure that had dogged them all the way, keeping a low profile and distance. He was now hiding in the bushes above the very path they were on.

Chapter 3
Educated Rivals

"Sometimes in the waves of change we find our true direction." [3]

On Dom's return home, Prue was pleased to get their share of the eggs.

"Goody-goody, Dommy," she exclaimed. "I was wondering what to have for tea. Where did you get these?"

"Oh, on the cliffs, Penlee way," said Dom. He just didn't feel comfortable sharing his secret place, even with Prue.

In another home, in neighbouring Cawsand, different news was being shared.

"Are you sure they were on Rame and they didn't find anythin'?"

"Yes, dad, all they was interested in was seagull's eggs. They didn't find nothin'."

Bruiser's eyes gleamed suspiciously. "You need to keep an eye on them, if you know what's good fer you." As he spoke his big fist hit Rydd in his chest, winding him. "I don't like it that they boys have started goin' over to Rame – so watch 'em."

---

[3] Quote unknown

At the Martyn's cottage Ned came in looking grim, "Where were you when I was lookin' for you today?" he grumbled at Dom. "You shoulda' bin working with me."

Dom squirmed. "I was out with Davy and Tris," he replied.

Ned glowered. "What you hobnobbin' with that pastor's son fer? They're not our sort; all holier than thou. Don't you go gettin' into religion, I won't have it. There ain't no God at all and if there were, he's done nothin' but harm in taking your mother."

Dom flushed and wanted to protect his friend but decided it was best to keep quiet.

Ned turned to Prue and began complaining about the poor pilchard catch that day. "It's no longer such regular catches. I'm thinking of changing my work," he said. Prue and Dom were surprised.

"What would you do?" asked Prue in a worried voice.

"I've got an idea; you'll see," he said mysteriously.

Later, Prue and Dom talked in his bedroom, wondering whatever ideas Ned might have for different work. At last, she said, "You'd best get to bed. It's school fer you tomorrow and mind you're polite to Mrs Trevelyan; without her it wouldn't be happening."

His heart sank; no more freedom. *Bother Mrs Trevelyan. Why didn't she mind her own business?*

He sighed as he got into bed.

The next morning, which was the first Monday in September, scrubbed by Prue, who had tried to tame his unruly hair, causing him to yell as she dealt with the tangles, Dom was met on the doorstep by a sullen Davy and off they went up the hill with plodding steps. Tris was waiting for them. The Chapel room had been divided into two by a screen. Little children were crying and being torn from tearful mums. Mrs Trevelyan, a serious woman with an angular face but kind eyes, was busy with the little ones, directing them inside, telling them, "Be sure to say 'Good morning' to your new master, Mr Crabbe."

Through the partition and into the gloomy room they went, hesitantly. Mr Crabbe, a tall, stern-looking man in a stiff collar and grey suit stood grimly, holding a cane by his side. Desks were in rows. About 15 children sat silent and stiff.

His grey eyes behind his pince-nez glittered dangerously. The boys were directed by his pointed bony finger to some vacant desks and sat down; with heavy hearts.

"You are just in time," Mr Crabbe said. His voice had no welcome, but rather, had an edge to it. Dom's heart chilled. Mr Crabbe laid the cane carefully on his desk for all to see. They were all told to give their full names and ages, which the master wrote in his register.

He worked along the rows asking their details. The girls across the gangway from Dom gave their names. The pretty one nearest him said in a sweet low voice, "Lamorna Stephens, 14 sir." He nodded approvingly.

Dom was surprised; he knew the name but she was not from Kingsand. At his turn he answered carefully: "Dominic Martyn sir, I'm 13–14 next month."

Suddenly, there was the sound of clumsy feet and in walked three boys. Dom gasped. It was Rydd Bolitho, who looked stormy and flushed. Directed to some places they sat sullenly.

"You're late, answer your names," rasped Mr Crabbe, pointing at the largest one of them.

"Herbie," said Rydd's first companion.

"Herbie is not a proper name," the master said sharply. "Give me your full name and age and you call me sir."

Herbie swallowed, "Herbert Wilcox, sir,14," he muttered, blushing red. Next came Richie Grills, half the size of Rydd and short with a narrow, pointed face and greasy red hair. He looked shifty and stuttered his name and age with an oily smile of embarrassment. A couple of girls and boys smirked at his stutter and suppressed a giggle.

"And you?" said Mr Crabbe imperiously, directing his gaze at Rydd.

"Rydd Bolitho, fourteen, nearly 15," he said loudly. Defiance was in his voice.

"Rydd?" replied the master acidly. "Is that your proper name?"

Rydd's eyes flashed, "Yes – that's my name." The words shot out like a challenge.

Mr Crabbe took his measure with a long look and fingered his cane. "That's my name – sir," he repeated, emphasising the 'sir'.

Rydd's eyes narrowed and he glanced at the girls suspiciously, daring them to laugh.

He looked like he was about to argue but, as the cane was grasped in the master's clenched fist, he chose to say "That's my name – sir." Rydd emphasised the last word with a spot of insolence. The master's mouth hardened. "You are at the top age for this school," he said, as though it was Rydd's fault. "But you have another year."

After an uninspiring talk by the teacher about how privileged they were and how grateful they should be to Mr and Mrs Trevelyan, there was a prayer and a verse from the large King James Bible on his desk. Mr Crabbe announced Colossians 3 verse 20 and read, "Children, obey your parents in all things, for this is well pleasing unto the Lord."

No one could miss the point of this verse about children obeying their parents in the Lord. Clearly, this was a warning from the teacher who was, as he explained, in place of their parents for the time they were in school. For all of Ned's lack of affection, Dom couldn't help being relieved that Mr Crabbe was not his father. No one could miss the point of "Children, obey your parents in the Lord for this is right."

So, the day got underway. Slates and chalks were given out and arithmetic followed. Dom immediately dropped his chalk, which rolled under Lamorna's desk. She reached down and picked it up, giving him a shy smile. Her green eyes looked kind. He thanked her and smiled back; his heart fluttered; he was smitten.

The day wore on monotonously. At lunch break they were allowed out briefly and wolfed down their bread. As he ate, Dom's eyes were drawn to Lamorna, who was skipping with her friends. As she jumped, her blonde hair danced in the sun and her cheeks flushed. He heard the sound of her delightful laughter, which ran up and down the music scale. *I must find a way to get to know her better,* he thought to himself.

Rydd and his two mates were huddled in a corner, keeping themselves apart, obviously making plans. Herbie was several inches taller and wider than Rydd, who was a fairly stocky guy himself. Richie seemed to be the weak third party of the trio and sidled up to them both. When he smirked, his front teeth were protruding and pointed, just like a weasel. As they lined up to go back, Dom was suddenly tripped up from behind and fell in the door. He turned to see Rydd behind him, grinning along with Herbie and Richie giggling. He felt foolish but there was no time to retort.

The long afternoon involved a map of Great Britain, which Dom found interesting, having never seen one before. Tris was quick at answering questions, provoking Rydd to whisper "Crawler," Richie hissed, "Teacher's pet." Tris ignored them but Mr Crabbe had heard.

"What did you say?" he demanded.

"Nuffin', sir," they said, Rydd looking wide-eyed and innocent.

"If you speak again when I am talking, you will feel this cane on your hand," he warned.

Rydd looked stormy, Herbie blushed and Richie looked scared.

At last, the bell went and out of the stale room they rushed, into the fresh air: they were free! Dom and his friends sauntered down to the beach, just behind Lamorna and her friends, Josie Pascoe, whose parents ran the grocery shop in Cawsand Square and Lizzie from the Ship Inn on Garrett Street. Dom noticed how the three linked arms with Lamorna in the middle; she seemed to be a good friend and was always popular with the other girls and never alone at break times. The sun was on the water but had passed over the hills behind, leaving pink cloud trailing across the late afternoon sky.

"That Lamorna is beautiful," Dom said dreamily, not noticing anything else.

"But she is a Stephens," said Tris. He stressed the surname. Dom looked blank until Tris continued, "They live just along from us. Her dad is Sid Stephens, and he is Bruiser Bolitho's right-hand man in everything, including smuggling. He's as mean as Bruiser is strong."

"Oh no," muttered Dom, he had paled.

Davy whistled. "That Rydd is a nasty piece of work, like his dad. He's not called Bruiser fer nothin'."

As the days progressed, Dom was interested in some of the school work but in Maths he often had a block. Mr Crabbe explained that two years ago, in 1816, the gold guinea had been replaced by the British pound. Dom had never even seen a guinea so it meant little to him. On one occasion they were set money sums with pounds, shillings and pence to add up. Mr Crabbe checked the pupils' work. When he came to Dom, "It's wrong," was all he would say. Dom did the sum again and had to take it out to the master's desk. "It's still wrong – do it again," rasped the master. Dom rubbed it out and started again. A third time Dom still had the same answer, so, feeling more confused, he made the journey out to the high desk of the teacher again. By now, everyone's interest was sparked: they were watching to see what would happen next. Rydd and Richie were delighted. Herbie was still struggling with his own work. Dom was nearly in tears as he laboured again over the complicated sum. Nervously, he went out the fourth time.

"Dominic, you, stupid boy it's still wrong!" Mr Crabbe's voice was full of exasperation. Everybody sat up at the tone of his voice. Dom's frustration erupted in a rare explosion. "It's not!" he shouted.

The class gasped. Rydd rubbed his hands in expectation. Mr Crabbe took up his cane and set his gimlet eyes at Dom. It was nearly break time.

"You keep missing the farthing." He pointed with his cane at the sum. "The answer is 21 pounds, 15 shillings, and threepence farthing. Now go back and correct it! You will miss your break time and do the sums I set you. Don't argue

with me again or you will get six strokes of this on your hand."
He gestured with his cane.

Dom slunk back to his desk, his face bright red, amidst many giggles from the others. When the master turned his back, a pellet hit Dom in the cheek. He looked across and saw Rydd just putting down his ruler which he had used to send it. He and Richie were grinning. *I hate Maths,* thought Dom furiously. He glanced at Lamorna and found she was smiling sympathetically. She mouthed the word 'sorry'; that warmed his heart!

In the weeks that followed, tension grew between Rydd and Mr Crabbe. Several months later, Rydd had grown really careless. He eventually fell afoul of the teacher when he was caught cheating. Mr Crabbe ordered him to the front and then, picking up the cane threateningly, instructed him to hold out his hand. Rydd was humiliated – the rest of the class were watching in tense silence and fear. It was important to save face and not to look a coward, so Rydd held out his hand, but his mouth was defiant. The cane swished through the air six times. Rydd flinched but bit his lips. He was in pain but he hadn't made a sound. Mr Crabbe appeared to enjoy the punishment; his face flushed with satisfaction. Rydd's face also flushed, but with anger, his dark eyes were full of hate.

"You can tell your mother and father about your behaviour," rasped the master.

"I'll tell my dad, I will." His voice was grim as he emphasised the last two words.

As they left school, Dom overheard him say, "You wait, Mr bloody Crabbe. I'll set my dad on you."

He stalked off down the hill with his two admiring mates patting him on the back.

From his home an hour later, Dom's attention was caught by a big shadow passing the window. It was Bruiser Bolitho, stomping up the hill to the school room. *Looks like trouble*, thought Dom and slipped up next door to Old Maudie's, where he could get a better view. Rydd's huge dad was built like a wrestler, his sleeves rolled up over hairy arms. He held a stick with which he banged on the chapel door. Mr Crabbe appeared and a loud altercation began. As Bruiser's voice got louder, so did his language become wilder. Amazed, Dom saw him hold the master up by his collar in his two beefy hands until the teacher's feet left the doorstep. He banged him repeatedly against the door.

"You bloody tyrant!" yelled Bruiser. "You hit my boy again and I'll kill yer!"

Mr Crabbe was wriggling like a fish on a hook. His pince-nez fell off and his eyes were bulging. "See if I don't," added Bruiser and, throwing him into the doorway, he stomped off.

Dom, who was unseen, had shrunk into Maudie's doorway. He saw Bruiser's neck was bright red and he was muttering obscenities. Even Dom, who was not involved, felt weak at the knees in the face of such rage. Maudie and Sol, having heard the noise, had been watching from their window and emerged from their door.

"Mark my words," Maudie prophesied in her reedy voice, "death is cummin' from that man. Evil's in the air all around 'im."

Sol nodded vigorously in agreement. Her tall and lanky son was a young man of few words. It appeared his brain had been partially damaged at birth. The irony was that he had been named after the Bible's most wise King, Solomon, but to all and sundry he was known as Simple Sol. He always seemed fond of Dom.

"Don't 'ee worry Dom, Sol'll look after 'ee," he muttered; a slight drool of saliva came from his mouth. Dom was surprised at both what Maudie and Sol had said. He thanked them and went home, pondering their words.

Towards the beginning of October, the sea reminded them of its malevolent power. The weather had changed, as though, in a sulky mood, it had tired of being an Indian summer. The temperature dropped and the gale tore in from across the Channel. White horses galloped in from the bay, flinging themselves upon the rocks with suicidal abandonment. Jan Noakes son Tim, aged ten, was fishing with his mates on the rocks just below Pastor Kenny's church. He was a bit of a loner, 'as thin as a rasher of bacon', the locals said. His mates grew hungry and fed up as they hadn't caught anything.

"We'm goin' 'ome," they said. "Comin'?"

Tim was a determined little lad and shook his head. As they were used to his stubbornness his two mates left him to it. It was high tide and the swell was rising high. Tim had to retreat a couple of times. The old saying was that every seventh wave was the big 'un. And so it proved. Tim, concentrating on his line, never noticed the giant green swell rising up. Higher up on the road, Ma Tresco was passing by, hunched over against the wind. She glanced down over the wall and saw the giant wave rearing up. And then, she spotted Tim. She saw what was about to happen and screamed at him, "Tim, boy, look out!"

He looked up, but too late. Ironically, her warning meant he never saw what was about to hit him. At that moment the wave broke over him and sucked him greedily off the rock.

Another wave took its place and he was gone, "jest like he never was there. One minute he was, an' the next, gone forever." Ma Tresco said, again and again, in re-telling her story. The body was never found. The whole village joined in the tragedy, trying to comfort his grieving parents. Pastor Kenny tried to help but they would have none of it. Bitterly, they said, "How could there be a God to do such a thing to a little boy?" There was no answer. The sea had won; as it often did.

Chapter 4
Rydd the Rival

The fishermen know that the sea is dangerous and the storm terrible, but they have never found these dangers sufficient reason for staying ashore. [4]

That October, Dom's 14th birthday was nearly totally forgotten, as the cold weather made life extra hard. Even Dom only remembered when writing the date at school. Mr Crabbe seemed different; less sure of himself. Dom noticed he never picked on Rydd again, who had boasted to all and sundry that his dad had taught the teacher a lesson! The classroom was not a happy place; their teacher was waspish and cutting in his words with anyone who made mistakes. The class laboured under a heavy negative atmosphere and had little incentive to do any more than the absolute minimum demanded of them.

Dom's birthday might have been no different to any other day except that Prue, suddenly remembering the date, made a special lardy cake, Dom's favourite. There was no money for presents, but Prue proudly brought in a bright red scarf she had secretly knitted. "To keep 'ee warm," she said, giving him

---

[4] Vincent Van Gogh

a big hug. "Happy birthday, dearest Dommy." Ned was nowhere to be seen and never returned from The Rising Sun until they were all in bed.

Now he was fourteen, surely Lamorna would take more notice of him! He looked for opportunities to smile and catch her attention, occasionally she smiled a gentle smile back. One day, his opportunity came. He was ahead of her as she was coming down the hill on her own because Mr Crabbe had kept her behind. She began to run fast but suddenly slipped on some mud and gravel and lost her balance. She fell sideways, her cloth bag flew through the air and its contents were strewn around. His heart jumped and he sprang into action. She sat on the ground, hugging her left leg. He saw a nasty graze and cut had caused the bleeding.

Calling for Prue to come, he ran over to her. "Hey, let me help you. Are you hurt bad?" he asked. He saw there were tears in her eyes.

"It's my leg," she panted. He took her arm and helped her up. Prue had appeared and quickly assessed the situation.

"Bring her over here," she called. "I'll get some warm water and a cloth."

"Oh my bag and things," she said looking back.

"Don't worry, I'll get them in a minute," he said. "Let's get you in first." She smiled weakly and he tenderly led her into his home. Dom had never been so close to her, as he led her limping over to their cottage. He felt proud, and a real man for the first time. He could hardly believe the lovely Lamorna was sitting on a chair in his own home! Prue tenderly bathed the graze and put something special on it, "To take away the sting," she said.

"You've bin very kind," Lamorna said in her gentle voice, "both of you," she added, turning her gaze upon Dom.

"It was nuthin'," he said, a bit embarrassed, "as long as you're alright."

She got up. "I must go, Dad will get angry if I don't get his tea. Thank you very much, Prue."

In her warm-hearted way, Prue gave her a quick hug. "Now you take care."

Quickly, Dom said, "I'll see you down the lane."

Together, they walked down. Dom felt he was walking on air; he didn't care that some passers-by were staring. He wanted this special time to continue. So, they went on, and began to chat about the awful Mr Crabbe until they reached the boundary. There she said, "You'd better not come any further. There'll be a row if my dad saw you with me. He'd punish me; he can get very nasty. Thank you so much, Dom. You were there at the right time to help me."

Dom wanted to hug her but didn't dare. Instead, he said softly, "I'll always want to help you, anytime. See you tomorrow."

He watched her slim figure go up the short hill. At the bend she turned and waved. He waved back. He sauntered home full of hope, going over all that had happened and every word she had said. Things were looking up!

At school in the next few days her friends had obviously noticed her leg and got the story out of her. They noticed his ongoing awareness of her and began to tease her, making her blush and they began to smirk and giggle whenever he was around. This embarrassed him and he withdrew a bit. Richie, always sneaking around, clearly got wind of this and wasted no time in sharing it with Rydd and Herbie. One break time they surrounded him while he was aiming to join Davy and Tris, who were kicking a ball around. Rydd's sneering voice mocked him.

"So, Dommy dummy, think you're special do ya?" Dom backed away.

Richie grew bolder because of this and began to chant, "Morna, Morna, Dommy's longin' for ya!" The others laughed. Dom, embarrassed, said. "Shut up, Richie!"

Herbie muscled in, dwarfing Dom with his bulk. "You little pukin' goody-goody; tell us to shut up again and I'll shut you up, with these!" Herbie raised his big fists, Richie giggled and Rydd grinned wolfishly, his teeth bared. Dom was intimidated and had decided to try and back off when, mercifully, the bell rang. His face was burning. Their jeering laughter followed him. Worst of all, Lamorna and her friends had been watching.

Christmas 1819 was also another low-key event at the Martyn household as there was little money for food and none for gifts. Prue did her best with a plum pudding, Aunt Letty sent over some sticky buns and Pastor Kenny kindly sent them a chicken, so they enjoyed a roast. Prue told Dom to keep quiet about who had donated it, in case Ned refused it. She told him it had been left on the doorstep.

A few days before, Dom had been racking his brains for a gift to give Lamorna. In the end, he searched through Prue's clothes drawer and, pushed away at the back, he found a small, prettily embroidered handkerchief, which he had never seen before.

She gave her permission, saying, "I see, my lad, you've got a soft spot for that girl. Go on. I never use it." He wrapped it in a piece of brown paper and wrote on it 'Happy Christmas

Lamorna'. He paused and then decided to go for it. He added 'love Dom'.

He saw Tris the next day, who thought it would mean future trouble but agreed, grinning at Dom's urgency, to slip it through the Stephen's door. A couple of days later Tris gave him some bad news. "I saw Lamorna yesterday Dom, and she had a bruise on her cheek. I think her dad hit her. They say he has a bad temper."

Dom was shocked, "Oh no!"

A moment later a thought struck him. "What if my gift caused her trouble?"

"It might not be that." Tris said to calm him but Dom was worried all over Christmas and there was no way to make contact with her. Tris had invited Dom to come to a Christmas carol service at his dad's church but Ned refused to let him go.

"You're not gettin' into no religion," he said, with his mouth set in a firm and bitter line. Dom wasn't really too bothered; being in a church would have been embarrassing, although he would have enjoyed being with Tris and being nearer to Lamorna who lived nearby. The Kenny's had family relations down from up-country so Tris was not free to spend time with Dom.

When term began in the new year, Mr Crabbe, to everyone's relief, was gone. The gossip was that he was too shaken by Bruiser's threats to carry on, especially with Rydd in his class. Mrs Trevelyan hired a lady from Millbrook. It was clear that Miss Jane was from a well-to-do home. A slim but tall lady and well-dressed, Miss Jane couldn't have been more different to Mr Crabbe. She held herself with authority and demanded respect. Wafts of perfume came from her as she swished up and down. The girls adored her. The boys quickly learned that she was not as weak as they at first thought. She was a good and inspiring teacher. In addition, Mr Trevelyan entered the room randomly at different times, clearly keeping an eagle eye on any who might take advantage. Rydd was the most likely to give trouble but, to everyone's amazement, he turned on the charm and appeared (at least in class) to be a changed character. He was quick to answer and swift to be a monitor, earning her approval. Dom, Davy and Tris were amazed but suspicious. Lamorna was one of her favourites and Miss Jane gave her much attention. Lamorna's honey-blonde hair cascaded, hiding her face, as she assiduously worked at every task, gaining good marks and praise.

Dom had taken the first opportunity to ask Lamorna if his gift had caused her trouble. She looked down and said quietly, "Yes, he found the paper with your note on it, flew into a temper, and lashed out cos you are not from our village. Don't worry, I'm used to it. But I have kept the hanky – it was beautiful, thank you."

"I am so sorry. The last thing I wanted was to cause you trouble." Dom didn't know what else to say. He hated Sid Stephens. *How could a father do that to such a lovely daughter?*

School continued at a relentless pace. Most days Rydd and his gang left school promptly, boasting and letting it be known that, now they were bigger, their fathers needed them to work and that their school days were numbered.

Dom found himself still more strongly attracted to 'Morna', as her friends called her. After the news of her being hit, he so much wanted to protect her, but it was hard to know how. Another difficulty was that on school days when he could see her, her friends were always with her. He loved her heart-shaped face and pretty green eyes; they were the deep emerald colour of the sea in the cove under Penlee. She began to feature in his dreams; always just out of reach. Davy and Tris teased him unmercifully. However, something else had been very disturbing to Dom as the school weeks continued. Rydd had clearly been making a play for her. Dom was sure it was partly to make him jealous. Dom tried hard not to show his feelings. Rydd had begun paying her much attention with his flashing eyes and his full red lips, readily smiling and making her laugh with his jokes. He had tamed his normally wild thatch of hair and even offered to share his pasty with her; although she refused.

One afternoon, Dom's heart dropped when he saw Rydd catch up with her after school and, playing the gent, offering to carry her bag. Dom could see from her face when she turned that she blushed bright red at something Rydd said. He was winning her! Dom's heart beat furiously with disappointment. How could she be so taken in?

The Easter holidays were a welcome break. Davy, Tris and Dom spent any free time, whenever their dads did not need them to work, exploring or swimming; when they could brave the cold water. Sol often joined them and was fearless at diving in, whatever the weather. It was extraordinary to see his prowess in the sea; he was in his element and didn't seem to feel the cold, despite his lean frame. The three lads explored the coast, and the rock pools; often they could be seen fishing off Penlee or Rame, without any incident and, further afield, they enjoyed rock-pools and shells on the endless Whitsands Beach.

After Easter, school work continued relentlessly. Dom struggled with Maths and English but enjoyed History, Nature study and all geographical work involving maps and other countries. The latter opened up a whole new world for him. Tris excelled at everything but remained modest about it. Davy struggled with most subjects and longed to be out of doors. There was some tension regarding Rydd who had begun, along with big Herbie, to bully younger boys and to flirt with all the girls. He scowled when he was near Dom or his friends. Mr Trevelyan's watchful presence generally kept things in check at the school. At last, after endless warm months of May and June when the whole class chafed at being indoors, Dom was given hope that the end might be in sight.

Prue had been constantly worried at their dad going out every evening and coming back later full of drink. "He be drownin' his sorrows but it's not good, Dom; he's wastin' our little money." Dom was concerned but more stirred by the fact that, just that morning, Ned had excited him by saying, "Now school will be over fer a few weeks, and yer time may be comin' to an end anyways. It's time you learned my trade, while it lasts. You're a'commin' out with me tomorrer."

At last! His dad was taking notice of him.

School broke up for the summer. Dom was relieved he no longer had to be in the same room as Rydd but he was going to miss seeing Lamorna. In other ways he nursed the hope he would be allowed soon to leave school – it depended on his dad and Mr Trevelyan. He hoped they would meet soon and talk about him.

On the first day of the holidays, Dom was shaken awake by Ned in the early dawn. With a slab of bread and cheese in his pocket and a jar of water in his hand, Dom was led by Ned down to Girt Beach. There was already a lot of activity and noise. Many boats were being launched. Davy's Dad, Sam, was giving orders. He was sturdy; a bigger version of his son. He had a florid face and bushy black whiskers. He was giving the orders in a voice that meant business. All his men buckled to. The boats were loaded with the seines, the big nets to catch the fish and the baskets, called mawns, were ready for storing the catch.

Dom was excited. The summer morning was still and fresh with the sky growing salmon-pink over Jennycliffe on the other side of the bay, causing the sea to flush like wine. One of the fishermen in Ned's boat, called Tom, took an interest in Dom and answered all his questions as they sailed out. The pilchard season was full on, he said, but not as good as in the old days.

"My father used to say there were so many fish in 'is day you hit 'em whenever you dropped yer anchor! But it's changin'; there seem to be less and less these days. It's worryin'." Dom was quiet, remembering Ned's comments the other night.

Tom continued explaining that they were still trading but that less salted fish went to France these days. They were selling more of them locally, as always in the past, in nearby Devonport market at Plymouth.

"How do the fish stay fresh?" asked Dom, remembering the stink of rotten fish on the beach.

"We salt them and when us gits back, the girruls will carry the mawns over to the palace."

"Palace?" repeated Dom. "Are they goin' to King George?"

Tom laughed out loud, "No, boy, that's the name of the cellars over there, where the fish be stored and cured with layers of salt to keep 'em fresh." He pointed to the large building about a hundred yards along the shore which had many holes in its wall. When Dom asked why were there holes, Tom told him it was to keep the pilchards cool.

"These nets are huge," Dom said. "Will there be enough fish to fill them?"

"Bless 'ee," laughed Tom again. "There be large shoals out there somewhere, we 'ope." He pointed as the boat lurched over the waves with Ned and several others rowing hard.

Out they sailed, over the pearly grey and pink sea, passing Penlee Point. Dom was bursting with excitement at being old enough to be with these tough seamen. He thought to himself, *I'm really growing up now.*

Way out towards the horizon stood John Smeaton's sturdy lighthouse. Previous attempts at building a lighthouse there had either been destroyed by storms or fire. The boat slowed and the men started to haul the nets over the side. The boat rocked on the swell. Dom had never seen the land from this angle before. The villages seemed so small. His beloved Rame was not far away, with its chapel still looking like a horn on the humpy head of a great sea-monster; but this time it was facing him. He was fascinated to be so far out on the swirling, emerald green water which was now sparkling in the warm morning sun. He wondered, *should they sink, would he be able to make it back to land?* He thought he might, as he was quite a good swimmer.

All the boats were spread out. It was not long before the nets were straining. "All hands pull 'em in," yelled Sam to his men. Dom was nudged by his dad to help haul them in. There was a rhythm to it: "Heave," they panted, "heave!"

Their brawny arms were straining; the boat was slanting over. At last, a large catch was landed, pilchards by the hundreds were flapping around with their mouths open and also there were crabs of varied sizes; a few jellyfish and a few mackerel. The small crabs and unwanted jellyfish were thrown back over the side. The men looked satisfied and there was lively talk.

A couple of hours later, after they had eaten their food, they rowed back. Dom was allowed to share Tom's oar. He felt important but it was demanding work. Gradually, as they passed Penlee, the village grew closer. As they arrived back in Kingsand, with other boats following, the beach was full of women and girls. By now, Dom's hands were blistered and his young arms were aching but he felt proud and grown-up. The mawn baskets, full of fish, were carried off by the women to the palace.

Dom was looking to his dad to hear some words of praise. Ned ignored him. Encouragement came from Tom.

"You bin a good lad; you'll make a fisherman one day, eh Ned?" Some of the other men patted Dom on the back. Ned only grunted and sent Dom home. "I'll be back later," he said.

Dom made his way up the Cleave, feeling flushed with his new experience, but inside he was longing for his dad's approval.

That evening there was much riotous laughing and shouting on the Green outside The Rising Sun. The fish had been sold and Bill Bray bought a huge amount to sell at his shop on the Cleave. The poor hung around to scavenge any scraps. Ned joined them and came home after dark, worse for wear. Prue searched his pockets as he snored. "A few coins at least," she whispered. "What a waste."

After this and subsequent days of fishing in which Dom had eagerly participated, Ned was in a bad humour. Dom was the butt of his temper. On the latest trip there had been a rougher sea and, with the motion as they rode the swelling waves, Dom had got seasick and messed up on the boat. When they got home, Ned ranted at him. "When will you grow up and be a man instead of a lily-livered waster?" he yelled.

Dom felt the sting of injustice and answered back. "It was only once – it was that rough sea!"

"Rough be damned," he swiped him with the back of his hand. A red weal came up on Dom's face. With hot tears of anger, he ran out of the house. He made for the cliff path and his safe place. Although Rame was a couple of miles away, there was nowhere better to be; to lick his wounds and recover his peace.

It had become hot and Dom was sticky with sweat. The late afternoon air was close and not fresh. The skies were hazy. As he paced the cliff path after Penlee Point, Dom's passion subsided. He began to enjoy the view of the bay and the boats sailing out from Plymouth. Rame loomed ahead, reassuringly solid, beckoning him. He hurried on, sweating but impatient to get there. Rame was slumbering in the afternoon heat; the haze blurred the horizon from view. A schooner, far out, disappeared ghost-like into a growing mist. Fishing villages, Looe and Polperro, were hidden within it. The wind of the morning had died down and the sea was wave-less now, shimmering silk. Some small boats lazily drifted around to search their lobster pots. The cliff sides were aflame with orange montbretia and sunny yellow gorse. The wild ponies moved slowly in the summer afternoon heat.

As Dom crossed the neck of land to get to the headland, he glanced down at the razor-sharp lines of jagged rocks some seventy feet below. Between each line were the pure, turquoise depths. The water was making very little movement. It seemed the tide was beginning to go out. He shivered at the thought of falling on to those rocks which again seemed to look up at him like rows of evil teeth.

Sweating heavily, he climbed the steep path to the top. He rested on the gaping window ledge of the chapel to catch his breath and fell again to thinking about his dad. Even earlier this morning, Ned had shouted at him for wasting water. Last night it was the wood he hadn't chopped properly. It seemed he could do nothing right in Ned's eyes. Here, on Rame, there was peace and space to think; home was tension, with an edge in the very atmosphere. *How long could he stand it? But where could he go?* Only dear Prue made it any way bearable.

The window ledge was hard. He dropped down and found a cool corner on the grass close by the chapel wall. His mind weary with thinking, he fell into a troubled sleep. He was awoken hours later by a thunderclap. To his amazement, as he jerked awake, it was almost completely dark. The sky was covered with menacing clouds, but the air was muggy and thick. Suddenly, livid lightning forked down through the clouds. As he looked out, he saw there was a hint of moon which was lying just on the bank of sea-fog, like a dull pearl. Every now and again there was some intermittent light in the gloom. He licked his lips; his mouth was dry and he was stiff. The first drops of rain began to fall.

Suddenly, he was jerked into attention by a surly voice somewhere below him. Who could it be at this hour? He heard another deep voice saying, "Git the lanterns ready."

He crawled to the edge of his grassy ridge to look down. There were three or four shadowy figures moving about. One was bigger than the rest. They were on a rocky outcrop fifty feet below him. A rough voice snarled, "You stupid idiot; give me the flint."

Dom's eyes widened; he knew that voice. It was Bruiser! Another voice came gruff and deep, "Bloody fog, I can't see what I'm a-doin'." It was probably Bruiser's mate, Sid Stephens, Lamorna's father!

Another rough voice answered, "Sid, stop moanin' and git over 'ere."

What on earth were they doing here in his secret place at night? Peeping over his ledge, Dom could just see, in the light of a freshly lit lantern being swayed from left to right, that the shadowy figures were carrying kegs. *Smuggling! Of course! That's what they were into!* There was often guarded talk of it amongst the fishermen with Davy's Dad, and Tris' words about Sid Stephens came back to him.

From out to sea came an answering flash of blue light from a large boat that emerged from the fog, heading towards them. Dom knew that big luggers like this occasionally came from Roskoff. Bruiser and his men had disappeared, going further down. As Dom watched and waited, he saw a couple of boats making their way out through the mist, towards the lugger which was now about a hundred yards out. They then returned, loaded with barrels and kegs so heavy that the boats were close to being submerged. Willing hands met the boats as they drew close and started carrying the contraband ashore.

Dom had seen enough; he needed to get away. Stealthily, he arose and darted into hiding around the chapel corner. In the dark, his foot stumbled and sent a shower of stones down the hillside, bouncing off the rocks. Shouts of alarm came from below.

Dom's heart was in his mouth as he ran, as carefully as he could, down the steep, uneven path. He was petrified of being caught. As he reached the neck of land, the bank of fog mercifully enshrouded him. He could not risk running straight up the hill to the road and some farmhouses as he might have, because he would be above the fog and in full view. Instead, he had to choose the more difficult cliff path which snaked off on his right into the foggy darkness. After a while, he stopped and listened, catching his breath. There was no sign of pursuit. There were many stumbles on the rough path in the misty gloom; he felt almost like a blind man; once or twice he wandered too near the edge and could have slipped down on to the rocks or sea. At last, he reached the welcome shadow of Penlee and then the cover of the woods. No one seemed to be following him. Progress was quicker then because the fog was dispersed by the trees. He ran home as fast as he could, risking the quicker route through a deserted Cawsand. He was sure trouble would await him, as he was so late.

Prue met him as he came in the door. She was in a state. Her little lace mop cap was all askew.

"Dommy! Where have you bin?" she asked, stressing the word 'have'. "You're so late! Have you got into trouble?"

"No. No!" he protested. "I was wandering around looking at the skylarks and fell asleep in the heat." He still didn't want even Prue to know about his secret retreat.

"Yer mash'n mince I cooked special is cold. You'd better eat it before yer dad gets in. He's out again at the pub. If 'ee gits hold of you and 'ee's the worse fer drink, he'll shake you to death."

Dom washed his hands, relieved that only Prue was home.

"You'd best get to bed. I'll bring yer food up. I'll tell yer dad you're poorly."

Late that night, still with no sign of Ned, Dom was awoken by the muffled clopping of hooves going up past his window. Without lighting the candle, he looked out from the side of the curtain. Lines of donkeys, loaded heavily with kegs and barrels, were making their ghostly way up the street. Men were leading them but making no noise nor talking. *It must be the contraband,* he realised. Prue slipped into his room; she had heard it too.

"It's the Cawsand smugglers," she whispered, "don't let them see you."

"Where are they going?" He asked.

"Susie Hancock and Daisy were tellin' me they are hiding the goods up somewhere around Maker woods. And some are taken to Millbrook for the gentry."

Susannah and Ray Hancock ran the grocer's shop just around the corner. It was a hive of information and news. Daisy was Bill Pollock's wife from the fish shop. She was a gossip, always complaining about the ever-present stink of fish in her house.

Prue continued in her quiet voice, "They say 'tis only a matter of time till the Searchers men catches Bruiser and his gang. Dad says they're fools, 'cos someone will blab on them."

The Searchers was the local name for the Revenue men who were charged to stop smuggling.

Dom stiffened at the mention of Bruiser. *So, this must be the goods he'd witnessed at Rame!*

"Why don't they hide them in Cawsand?" He asked.

"They're clever. They've stopped usin' Cawsand Beach and the tunnels up St Andrews' street cos the Searchers have bin around pokin' their noses in and askin' too many questions, so Aunt Lettie says."

"Is Dad in yet?" he asked, to change the subject.

"Yes, he fell asleep in the chair from the drink. I told him you was poorly."

He lifted the corner of the curtain again. The long line of donkeys was coming to an end and at the back was the stocky figure of Rydd, his unmistakable mop of hair, partly covered by a man's cap slung on the back of his head, hanging over his eyes. He was prodding the donkey viciously with his stick. Dom froze and dropped the curtain before he could be spotted.

Chapter 5
A Dangerous Discovery

"The sea knows no limits, makes no concessions. It has given us everything and it can take everything away from us." [5]

After an Indian summer, with lots of swimming and local adventures for the three friends, the Autumn chill had set in. The few trees in the village were turning golden. School had resumed. Davy was no longer at school now as he was required full-time by his dad. Dom wished that Ned would say the same.

Dom's fifteenth birthday was a few weeks away. One day, on which Tris had not appeared, they were allowed at lunch break to take their snacks up to Minnadew and run wild on the grassy slopes and up into the Maker woods. Rydd, built strong and muscular like a young ox, showed off his powers on the games. He flirted with Lamorna and her friends, making jokes and giving out some of his sweetmeats; often glancing over to see if Dom was looking. If he was, Rydd grinned mockingly and raised his fist. Dom felt a new stab of jealousy. While she was friendly to him in a distant, general way, he longed for

---

[5] John Ajvide Lindqvist

more than the beautiful smile which lit up her face. He couldn't compete with muscular Rydd, who, with his supportive mates, big Herbie and slim, smirking Richie Reynolds, was play-wrestling. Richie was the opposite build to big Herbie and seemed to lack any of Rydd's glamour. His greasy red hair was plastered to his forehead as though with oil. Rather like a chameleon, Richie seemed to be fawning on Rydd, laughing at his jokes and echoing the things he and Herbie said. Both of their families were entwined with Rydd's father, Bruiser. Herbie's father was a right-hand man to Bruiser in the clandestine contraband, as was Jack Grills, Richie's dad, who provided a base.

Unlike slick mover Rydd, Herbie, a bulky overweight lad, was clumsy and lumbering in his movements but made up for it by sheer size and his ability to lift large and heavy weights. Again and again, Rydd emerged the victor because he was not only strong but a quick mover; and had big Herbie as a sort of minder to back him up. Lamorna and her friends couldn't help being impressed. One of the younger boys had brought a rough ball which he didn't keep for long as Rydd and the bigger lads muscled in, kicking it around. Dom enjoyed football and joined in and, at one point booted it up by mistake, into the woods and ran after it, shouting "I'll go!"

He didn't see Rydd react like lightning to follow him. Searching the undergrowth, Dom suddenly discovered a cave partly hidden by branches. Intrigued he began to pull at them but before he could look inside, a shadow fell over him.

"What d'you think you're doin?" The harsh voice carried a grim threatening tone. "Get out of here," he continued.

A memory of that snaking voice when he was walking with Prue, years ago, flashed across his mind. As Dom straightened up, Rydd, checking with a swift glance behind him that no one could see, came at him with his fists up. Dom, caught by surprise, and intimidated by the force coming at him, was no match against him. Rydd's hard fist struck him right in the stomach, knocking the breath right out of him. In shock and pain, he bent over. As he did, 'whack' a second upper cut smashed into his jaw. Blue and yellow stars exploded in his head and he fell flat on his back in the undergrowth. Rydd stood over him, his face like thunder; the black eyes glittered murderously.

"Git goin' and don't ever come 'ere again or I'll kill ya. An' if you tell any of your mates about this place, they'll get it too."

There was no mistaking the determination on his face; he meant it. Rydd turned and strode away quickly. After a few minutes, feeling sick, Dom staggered to his feet, his jaw throbbing. He stumbled back down out of the woods, feeling shocked and ashamed of his cowardice. Richie was hovering in the near distance, watching. In his dazed state, Dom was slow to realise that Richie was appointed as a sentry to make sure that Dom came out quickly. The teacher had come and rung the bell, ordering everyone back to class. Only Richie lingered nearby, but Rydd was watching his exit from the gate at a distance. *Now,* he realised, *he had found the probable hiding place of some of the smuggled goods.* Thoughts darted through his mind. *But was his life now in danger? What could he do?* If he told anyone, the Bolithos would know it was him. Once he had started back, they slunk away, confident he was following. He glanced across and saw Richie smirking at him.

After school Rydd and his cronies were quick to leave, but went up the hill and Dom saw them standing near the gate to

Minnadew, ensuring that Dom did not explore the woods again. He went down the hill; his jaw was still aching, and he was dogged by an overriding feeling of failure and weakness. Now they knew that he knew something of their secret: *What might happen next?* He felt trapped.

The next morning in the early dawn, after a restless night, Dom arose before anyone else was up. The dreaded easterly wind was blowing strong and the sky was an angry red. The old saying "Red sky in the morning, sailors warning" automatically went through his mind. He stole out of the house and up to Minnadew, which was deserted. Making sure he was unseen, he slipped up into the woods, now gloomy and full of shadow. With difficulty he found the cave. The branches were gone. The cave was about twenty yards deep. Crouching down he stepped into the gloom. It smelt dank and musty, apart from a few twigs and stones it was completely empty; there was no sign of any contraband.

He began to make his way out. Still crouching, as he went, his attention was caught by a small amount of fresh brown dust. It wasn't dirt. He knelt and sniffed; it was tangy. He put in his finger and licked it cautiously. It was tobacco! So, contraband had been here! Satisfied, he emerged slowly, checking there was no one in the vicinity. All was clear.

Back at the house, Dom took his slab of cheese and bread as Prue appeared with the old brown teapot.

"You were up early," she said.

Dom grunted and ate hungrily. The wind whistled up from The Cleave through their Back Lane, causing their doors to creak and making the windows rattle.

"It's goin' to be a wild day," she said, putting down the teapot and pouring his tea. He drank thirstily. "We've got the south-easter. Yer dad's already gone to Sam to plan their day. I hope they will choose to be careful and stay fishin' local."

"Mm," he agreed.

After breakfast, calling out to Prue that he was going to see the waves, he left the house. The wind whipped through the narrow alleyways, causing buckets to roll around. A woman hurried past, hunched over and gripping her hat firmly as her coat flapped around her.

At the Cleave it was wild; the wind was in full force, tearing at his clothes. Out in the bay the high-tide waves were like an army of white horses racing in to break on the shore, invading the beach like a battleground. As they rolled in, the waves were high and slamming into the stone wall outside Davy's house, showering spray and shingle on to the road. Sailor Sam was sheltering in the porch entrance of the Devonport Inn, which was a popular pub on the Cleave, smoking his pipe. Dom hunkered down beside him.

"This 'ere wind is trouble," muttered old Sam.

His gnarled hands gripped his pipe. His face was lined like tree bark and his skin was tanned like leather from years at sea.

"That there breakwater they'm buildin' out yonder is changin' the current and takin' away our beach."

Dom was surprised but he had noticed the sand seemed less these days.

"They shouldn't be messin' with nature," grumbled the old man.

"Sam," asked Dom, "what happens when smugglers are caught?"

"The Revenue men will take 'em to court in Bodmin and they'll probly git jail; or they may git five yers in the navy."

Dom was shocked but before he could ask more, a nearby clock chimed nine.

He jumped up. "Oh, sorry Sam, I need to get off to school." With a hurried 'goodbye' he raced back up the hill, with the wind propelling him.

As he entered the school room, his stomach was in knots about facing Rydd again. To his immense relief, Rydd was absent. However, Rydd had obviously boasted of his victory, for the girls were smirking at Dom's entry; even Lamorna averted her eyes. Dom wondered what reason Rydd had given for the conflict and what lies may have been told, but he got no news. The boys avoided him. Tris was sympathetic as Dom told him that he was suddenly attacked by Rydd, the day before.

"I wish I had been there to defend you," said Tris.

Dom let him think that Rydd had just taken his opportunity to beat Dom up. He could hear Rydd's threat ringing in his ears.

It was better not to tell Tris about the cave and what might have been there, in case it endangered Tris as well as him. "Dom," said Tris determinedly, "after school, I am going to teach you how to box, like my dad taught me. You need to know how to defend yourself."

After school they gathered on the green outside The Rising Sun and Tris made him put up his fists to protect his face and chest and made boxing jabs at him. He taught him how to dance up and down on his feet to dodge the blows and how to make a right-hand jab. Dom gradually improved and got the hang of it. Tris was pleased with him.

The lads said goodbye then, as Tris had to be back to do jobs for his dad. The wind was raging as Dom made his way down the hill, trying out his boxing moves. As he reached the last right-angle bend before the lane opened out on to the Cleave, he could hear shouts and screams. He ran around the bend and, buffeted by the full force of the wind, he found a crowd clustered around the cottage at the sea's edge where the widow, Mrs Lundy, lived. He was shocked to see the back end of the cottage had broken off and fallen into the sea. The house looked jagged and torn like a broken tooth. Wooden struts were flapping in the wind like the wings of wild birds.

Ma Lundy was on the beach, surrounded by several women who were helping her pick up pots and pans, a stool, some sticks of furniture and some half-broken crockery. A teapot was floating incongruously on a wave and suddenly thrown on to the beach. Amazingly, it seemed intact. One of the women ran forward to pick it up before the wave crashed in again.

"My kitchen," Ma Lundy was wailing. "My 'ouse! What am I to do?"

Dom felt sorry for her. As he looked back at the cottage, he realised that the waves had ripped away some of the foundation stones on which her home had rested. He saw that Prue was already there comforting her.

He looked out to sea. The sky was a stormy grey, with torn scudding clouds racing across the sky like tumbleweed. Out across the bay, a sheet of rain was advancing fast, like an ominous, grey curtain. His eyes were watering in the cold wind. He saw some boats nearby being jerked up and down like bobbing corks.

"No fishin' today," said a voice close to him. It was Ned with his boss Sam. "We'll try tomorrer," Sam answered.

Ned was clearly in a bad mood as there would be no work, and no work meant no money. He turned and his eye fell on his son.

"Come on 'ome," he shouted above the wind. "I need some logs chopped."

Later, when they were all at the table, Prue told them Ma Lundy had been taken in by Bill and Daisy Pollock at the pub until another place could be found for her.

Dom's fifteenth birthday was a Saturday, which was also the fifth consecutive day of the relentless south-easter, but Prue was determined to remember it this year and tried to make it special. She presented him with the grand lardy cake, his favourite. She cut a generous slice.

"This so to fatten you up; you're too thin." She said giving him a hug.

Ned appeared. Prue had obviously reminded him, because he managed to say gruffly, "Have a good day."

He always avoided saying 'Happy Birthday' to Dom because it brought back too many bitter memories of Dom's birth and his own loss. He hurried out as Sam Pethick had sent for him. The storm had apparently brought larger shoals of fish nearer the coast and many boats were launching out on the stormy seas to fish within the lee of Penlee Point. They first had to overcome the unusually large breakers thundering on the shore.

Prue had been hiding something under her apron. As she shyly brought out a narrow package.

"Happy Birthday from Dad and me," she said, giving him a kiss on the cheek and a hug.

He unwrapped the rough paper and there, inside, was a long pouch. He loosened the pouch string, wondering what it was, and then gasped as he drew out a telescope!

"Wow!" he said, "this is wonderful! How did you manage this?"

"Well, it's not new, as you can see, there are some scratches. But I was talkin' to Sailor Sam about your birthday and wonderin' how we could afford anythin' at all, and he told me to wait while he went indoors and he brought out this pouch and said, ''Ee's a good brave lad, giv' 'im this from you and Ned.' I was so choked I could 'ardly speak! He so wanted you to have it and said it was to be from all of us; so there 'tis."

Dom was overwhelmed. He turned it over and over in his hand.

"It's the bestest present I've ever had! I've always wanted to look out to sea and watch the birds n stuff."

He held it up to his eye right away, looking out the window and down the street. To his amazement he could see right into Granny Ansty's room at the bottom where the lane turned. Then he turned it up the hill to The Rising Sun and got a close-up of a man rolling in a barrel of beer. Although the man was a good hundred yards away, he could see every detail, even the hairs on his arm.

"Wow!" he exclaimed again. "Amazin', everything's so big through this. This is the best birthday present ever."

He hugged his sister and did a little jig around the room. Her face lit up in the reflection of his joy.

He couldn't wait to go down and try it out in the bay. As he rounded the corner, the wind took his breath away. The sea was heaving and the foaming grey waves were throwing up quite large pebbles on to the Cleave, which was now covered with shingle, seaweed and stones. After aiming his telescope at Penlee Point, he could see all the details of the shelter and there was the lighthouse out on the horizon, looking half as close again. He could see some of the fishing boats in the bay and everyone on them – he was looking for Ned but couldn't really see him properly as he was leaning over the other side of the boat with the nets.

The houses had some bags of sand at their doors to prevent the encroaching sea from entering. Sailor Sam wasn't at his usual place but, as Dom went further down The Cleave, he saw him sheltering from the wind behind a higher wall at the far end. His beloved pipe was still firmly gripped in his teeth but the smoke was being whipped away by the wind.

As he reached him, Dom held out the telescope. Sam's face creased into yet another set of wrinkles.

"Thank you so much, Sam," said Dom. "This is so kind of you. I don't know what to say – it's the bestest present I've ever had."

Sam patted his arm. "It was my trusty 'scope for yers and yers. You be welcome, my lad. I ain't got no need now; me eyes be failin' anyhow."

Dom excitedly raised his telescope over the top of the wall.

"Wow!" He exclaimed, "I can see the new breakwater wall, as close as can be! It's a wonder, that's what it is."

"I'm glad 'ee be pleased my boy."

Thanking him again, Dom rushed around the corner and in minutes was letting Davy have a go with it. Davy had been stopped by his dad from going out in the rough seas. He was well impressed.

"Wait till Tris sees it," said Dom.

For the rest of the day Dom tried to dodge the heavy showers and wandered around the village. All the lanes were a swamp with mud. Opposite Hancock's, the grocers, he stopped by the lower protecting sea wall and levelled his telescope over at the Cawsand cottages backing on to the sea along Garrett Street. He wondered if he would see Lamorna but no one was about in the wild weather. It was pouring again and he was getting soaked, but he was entranced with his new gift. He aimed at Pastor Kenny's house and was amazed again at how enlarged everything was. He could see in the windows but there was no sign of Tris. As he moved it a little, there was Pastor in his church! Dom could see his head of grey-white hair and the Pastor's face with his specs on his nose. It was a kind face. Dom fell to wondering what was he really like? As a son, Tris seemed really fond of his dad and learned a lot from him. They must talk together a lot, unlike him and Ned. Perhaps Pastor Kenny wasn't as bad as Ned and some others thought. But this religion thing was a problem; and the fact that the Pastor was part of 'the other side'. Apart from seeing Tris as much as he could, perhaps it was best to keep his distance. He had enough trouble from Ned as it was.

He arrived home; his clothes sodden. That night, flushed with the success of his new present, Dom fell into a deep sleep but his dreams were dark. Again, he was falling from a height into a foaming, raging ocean. A weight was on his back. The waters engulfed and enclosed him. Air! He gasped at the sudden chill. Down, down the weight forced him. All was green and dark. He writhed and struggled to free himself from the terrible grip – something was wrapped tight around his legs – he was drowning… Suddenly, he fell out of bed with a shock, his legs and feet entangled in the sheets. Lying on the floor, he gradually came to. It wasn't real! It was that nightmare again. Relief flooded him but his heart was still pounding and still the memory was vivid. *What was it all about? Why was it happening again and again?*

The next morning, he was hot and feverish. His body was aching and he kept trembling. Prue called him to go fishing with Ned but when he didn't answer she came in and saw the state of him. His throat was parched, even his eyes ached, he told her.

"You've got a fever Dommy," she said, "I'm getting Dr Grey."

He tried to protest but didn't have the energy. Dr Grey was a well-respected gentleman who lived up the top of Fore street, where the houses were more impressive. He had his house built for him years ago. Ned, who was in a hurry, was annoyed with his son. Prue defended him.

"But he's really poorly, Dad. He's not puttin' it on. I'm goin' to get Dr Grey."

She ran out, bumping into Old Maudie and Sol, telling them about Dom. Sol was worried and upset saying "Poor Dom, poor Dom" over and over again; alternately he was wringing his large red hands and biting his nails.

Maudie went to get some herbal tea. She was an expert at local herbs and infusions. She went up slowly with it to Dom's room, muttering about her painful knees.

She gave Dom the tea infusion and stayed to make sure he drank it. He was grateful: it was pleasant and soothing.

"What's 'appening?" she asked sharply.

He found himself telling her all about his dream.

"How often have 'ee had it, me 'andsome?"

He told her and her eyes narrowed.

"It's a warnin' me lad, it's a warnin'. You need to be careful near the sea."

She continued, "I see dark clouds whirlin' towards 'ee."

Maudie often got visions and was ridiculed by some in the village, who called her 'dotty'. In some places she might have been put to death as a witch but the Cornish had a respect for the supernatural.

"What does it mean?"

"It means someone is workin' evil against 'ee. Who be your enemies?"

Before he could answer there were footsteps on the stairs and Dr Grey came into the room, bringing an air of calm efficiency. He greeted Maudie and then, after laying his cool hand on Dom's clammy forehead, he took Dom's hand and felt his pulse, at the same time taking out his silver pocket-watch to measure it.

"Open your mouth, son," he ordered, "and say 'Ah'!" Dom complied.

Dr Grey was a distinguished-looking gent with greying hair; smartly dressed in a shirt, tie and a silk waistcoat.

"Well, my lad you have been out in the rain a lot; getting soaked, I gather?"

Dom admitted he had.

"You've caught a chill: It's not too serious. I'll give you some medicine to bring your temperature down and to help keep your lungs clear. You should be alright in a couple of days." He paused and smiled. "As long as you take some rest and don't go out getting wet again too soon!"

He turned to Prue. "Let me know if he has any further complications but I think he'll be alright. He's young."

"Thankee', Doctor," Prue curtseyed, but looked worried.

Outside on the landing she said, "Doctor, will the medicine cost much? We have no spare coins."

He patted her arm. "Don't you worry, I'll pay," he said kindly, "I know the pilchard trade is mixed these days."

A load lifted off Prue with these words and she thanked him profusely as he departed.

That evening, as Dom laid in bed taking some broth Prue had made for him, he heard his dad come in and another voice speaking. Then Prue gave a cry.

A voice boomed up the stairs, "We'll take him up to Doctor, don't 'ee be frit." The deep tones were Ned's boss, Sam Pethick.

Whatever had happened?

Dom heard the door bang and looked out the window to see Ned hunched over in pain, clutching his arm, and being led by Sam and Matt, another mate.

Shortly afterwards, Prue rushed in.

"Now Dad's been in an accident," she cried. "He's smashed his arm and shoulder. First you – now him; it's one thing after the other."

"What happened?" asked Dom.

"The boat was caught by a gert wave and it threw him so he fell against the side and smashed hisself."

"Oh Dommy," she cried. "Whatever are we to do? He can't work like that!"

It seemed to Dom, as Prue had said, that there was one trouble after another, which spoiled the happy memory of the previous day. How things could change in twenty-four hours!

Later, Ned was brought home. Dr Grey had given him something to alleviate the pain and had bound his arm and shoulder up.

Dom took himself downstairs as Ned sank slowly into a chair. "That's it, I'm done. I've decided, this clinches it."

"What d'you mean, Dad?" They both asked in unison.

"I bloody well can't work on the boats anymore and in any case the pilchard trade is sufferin'." His face was lined with pain and worry.

He continued, "I've heard they're buildin' cottages over on Penlee for coastguards who can help the Searchers keep watch on the smugglers. It's a good look-out to watch Bolitho's boats and others commin' in. I bin thinkin' about it for some weeks. I'm goin' to apply. Dr Grey says he will speak for me to the Revenue."

Dom gasped and Prue looked scared. Many Cawsand villagers would hate him for this; especially Bruiser Bolitho's gang! Dom's thoughts were coming thick and fast. *What would Bruiser do when he found out? And Rydd!* This could put Dom in greater danger, he would be a bitter enemy. Then there was Lamorna, she'd hate him; he'd never stand a chance now, any hope of winning her was out of the window. His heart failed him.

By total contrast, Prue was sounding relieved. "This means a reglar' wage, Dad!"

"And a better house," said Ned. He was looking drained. "I need to sleep," he muttered. "Doctor Grey gave me somethin' to help." With that he was off to bed.

Dom and Prue stayed talking over this news. At least there would be regular money for food and clothes. They had heard there were already coastguards keeping watch further back on the coast towards Plymouth.

"The trouble is," said Dom, "coastguards are hated by so many. We won't be popular over that way." He had to keep his personal experience with Rydd from her. Rydd's murderous threat was never far from his mind.

As far as Cawsand was concerned, they knew that the whole village kept mum about the smuggling in strong Cornish loyalty and, in distrust of them, to stand against the authorities. Many of them provided tunnels and secret cellars to store the contraband until it was dispersed. Even Kingsand folk wouldn't give anything away and some of the so-called 'respectable' gentry kept the secret, enjoying their brandy and baccy.

"But there is a good thing," Dom added, looking brighter, "that we'll be outside of the villages and away from some of the Cawsanders' feelins against us." He had also realised that another positive thing was that he would be even nearer his beloved Rame, if they lived in Penlee woods.

Chapter 6
Witness to a Murder

"There is a thin line that separates life from death, but once it's crossed, it becomes as large as an ocean, and so treacherous that it's impossible to cross back."[6]

The Autumn of 1820 had rolled on with another strong sou-easter. It had stripped the trees bare of their leaves. Through November, the Martyns waited to hear about Ned's offer to the Revenue. Ned had warned them against saying a word to anyone. Neither Prue or Dom needed the warning.

The winter damp and chill had stolen in, sometimes blanketing the village with sea fog, so that any horizon was shrouded from sight and the world seemed to close in on them all. Sometimes the Cornish drizzle fell incessantly, day after day, until everything smelled of damp. The lanes were a quagmire. By collecting branches from Maker woods and using them only in the evenings with a couple of their few logs, they kept their cottage somewhat warm.

Prue knitted furiously, unravelling Dom and Ned's worn-out jumpers and making blankets, scarves and woolly hats to

---

[6] Federico Chini

keep out the cold. Ned's arm and shoulder ached badly. Dr Grey said he thought he had a fractured shoulder and arm, although he said he thought it was mending well. Ned was like a bear with a sore head, as he was limited from doing much at all with only one arm. Neighbours, aware of his inability to provide, dropped provisions in, often leaving them on the doorstep. This was where the village community worked well to help each other. Grocer Ray Hancock kept them supplied with a regular loaf of bread. His wife, Susie, had a heart for Prue and would frequently appear for a gossip and to bring some butter or a cake she had baked. Sam Pethick sent Davy around most weeks with some pilchards and other fish; and so, they survived. Prue made blackberry and apple pies from the berries in the hedges and 'fallers' stripped from the apple trees that Autumn. Dom helped her when he was not at school.

School continued endlessly. A few weeks earlier Dom had been cheered by the thought that his dad might be planning to speak to Mr Trevelyan and say that he would be needing Dom to leave school and work with him in the pilchard trade. But now, due to his dad's accident, all that was impossible. At least Miss Jane was a good teacher and order was kept and reinforced by the frequent appearance of Mr Trevelyan, who sometimes stood at the back of the room and sometimes was listening through the door from the other room. What he didn't see were the many times that Rydd and Herbie made sly comments against Dom and Tris. Dom's slate mysteriously disappeared and reappeared later with a bad split and crack. Fortunately, he could still use it. Another time his pencil kept going missing and ended up snapped in two. Tris even had work mislaid 'by accident' as Richie was collecting the slates for the teacher. Rydd especially was clever at keeping his misdemeanours hidden, which included regular cheating. He charmed Miss Jane and flirted, whenever he could, with Lamorna.

Since his fifteenth birthday Prue had been pleased to notice Dom was filling out; his back was broader. That morning, Dom had realised there were even a few whiskers beginning to form on his top lip and his body hair was growing; he began to feel really grown-up. He combed his hair more carefully nowadays. If only Lamorna would notice!

Through December the skies remained leaden and heavy but, now that the sou-easter had died down, the December frost had come, bringing freezing temperatures on the first day of the month. The only brightening news was that Ned had been accepted for the job and they were to move after Christmas into one of the coastguard cottages. Prue was excited and pestered Ned to find out about the sort of rooms they might get. There was, he told her, one main room and a kitchen downstairs with a scullery to wash in and do the laundry. There were three bedrooms upstairs and even a bit of garden, which they had never had before.

The other bright thing for Dom was his precious 'scope. It was his most treasured possession. With it, when the weather allowed, he had watched the break-water being built. It was looking higher and much wider now. He could see, up close, the activity and even the labourers working on it. He used it most days after school and had shared it with Davy and Tris, who were fascinated with what they could see.

On the dry days after school when Davy wasn't out working on the boats, he and Tris met up with Dom and, either explored the coastline past the Palace, or tramped over Minnadew and up the steep wooded hill to Maker. One day it was just too cold and wet to be outside. Tris invited them to his house.

"My dad says you can come and we'll play draughts, or I'll teach you chess."

Dom had never got up close to Pastor Kenny and was nervous. Dom and Davy turned up into Garrett Street, rival territory, but due to the freezing weather, the street was deserted. At the Manse, just off the street and adjoining the church building, Dom knocked and Tris opened the door. They entered into a warm house with nice wallpaper, clean paintwork and some solid pieces of oak and mahogany furniture. For both of them this was a big surprise. Home for them was never like this! They nudged each other and gaped. There were even pictures on the walls in proper frames! Later, Tris told them his father had inherited some wealth from his relatives. Now Tris led them through to a door at the end of the passage.

"This is Dad's study," he explained, knocking on the door.

Dom froze. It opened and, in front of him, was a man of medium height with a smiling face, bright blue eyes and a shock of grey-white hair. He was clean-shaven but with long whiskered sideboards.

"Come in lads," his voice was deep but warm. They entered and were mesmerised. They had never seen so many books! They lined all four walls. A large Bible was open on the desk in front of the window which looked out on some rocks towards the sea and he was clearly working on some sheets of paper; a plume was in the inkstand. His glasses were in his hand.

"Sorry, dad, we're disturbing your sermon," said Tris.

"Not at all. Any friends of yours are friends of mine," he answered generously. "I've heard a lot about you – which is Dom and which is Davy?"

Dom's mouth had been wide open in amazement. He found his voice and introduced himself. He found he was shaking hands in a warm and manly grip. Davy followed, reddening furiously.

"Well lads," Pastor continued, "I'm sure you're welcome and I'm also sure that, like Tris, you're always hungry. Tris," he turned to his son, "Tris go and find them some buns or lardy cake and enjoy the game-boards."

They mumbled their thanks and trooped out. As they went, Dom's eyes were attracted to a large, framed portrait of a good-looking woman on the wall. Tris noticed his glance and said sadly, "That was my mum. She died when I was a small boy."

"I never knew mine at all," Dom said in sympathy. Tris squeezed his arm in response.

They passed into another room which actually had a ruby-patterned carpet on the floor. Dom and Davy were only used to bare floors at home with the usual rag rug. The whole experience affected Dom deeply. In Pastor Kenny he saw a completely different type of father to any he had ever known. He envied the easy relationship Tris had with his father. *So, this is what it could be like,* he thought. Pastor Kenny didn't seem to fit the general gossip he had heard, nor the jaundiced view of him that Ned or the village had. He couldn't help feeling envious. Tris was so lucky!

After they had spent a good time on the games, it was time to go. Davy and Dom were walking home; sharing their amazement over the experience. On the corner of The Cleave they met Sol who was looking deadly serious, shaking his head and mumbling.

"I seed it – I did – I seed it." But they couldn't get him to tell them what he had seen. Eventually, they gave up as it was so cold. It was probably just another of Sol's funny turns.

Dom patted his arm and said, "Don't worry, Sol, it'll be alright."

Davy made his farewell.

As soon as he got in, Prue pulled him into the scullery. "You'll never guess what's happened!"

Prue had heard it all from Sue Hancock, who had got it from Mrs Trevelyan when she came into the shop. Apparently, a gentleman relative was expected to visit Mrs Grey; it was thought he wanted to bring an early Christmas present. He was known to be a wealthy lawyer from Plymouth. Mrs Grey had been anticipating his visit with some excitement, as most of the village knew. It was rare for anyone of wealth to enter their sort of village. He was bringing Christmas gifts and was due to stay a night or two. He was late arriving, but that was not unusual. The short winter daylight had given way to a damp, dark evening with the freezing fog on the high ground.

"But he never arrived, Dom." Prue's voice was breathless.

She continued the story, with Dom hanging on her every word. Later that evening, a man coming along the top road from the nearby village of Millbrook, stumbled over something in the lane. In the light of his lantern, he was shocked to see it was a gentleman with blood on his face and whiskers, who had clearly been wounded in his head.

"The man was dead, Dommy! His horse was grazing nearby. The gentleman's wealthy silk waistcoat looked torn and a broken watch-chain dangled from it."

It turned out that the man had put the body on his horse and made his way to Dr Grey's house, not knowing that he was bringing him the body of the expected visitor.

"And, oh Dom," Prue's eyes were pained, "poor Mrs Grey answered the door, expecting her relative, but, when she saw his body, she screamed and collapsed in a dead faint!"

Prue's eyes were filled with tears. Dr Grey, who was fortunately at home, had apparently quickly taken charge of the situation.

Dom was shocked. At that moment, Ned came in the front door. The news had passed speedily through the village and he had heard it. Everyone was shocked and sorry for poor Mrs Grey.

"It must have been some wild thieves from a nearby village," said Dom.

"It's more than thieving!" said Ned grimly. "It's murder!"

As he went to bed that night, Dom was thinking about the tragedy when he suddenly remembered Sol's words. He had said, "I seed it."

Sol would never do such a thing. Sol would never normally hurt a fly. But he had seen something. What had he seen?

Next morning early, he called on Sol but he looked scared and all he would say was "I ain't sayin'. I don't want them to get me."

Despite Dom trying to draw him out with questions, his mouth was set in a firm line. Dom tried to encourage him to talk to Dr Grey but this made him worse.

"I can't. I can't!" he refused, moaning. He turned away burying his long thin face in his scarf and pulling his wool hat down over his head.

At school the story was all the rage. Lizzie Hoskins again had the news hot from The Ship Inn. After school that day, the three friends were down on the rocks looking in the rock pools for crabs. After a while Davy stood and stretched. He looked up at Minnadew.

"Hey," the tone of his voice caught their attention and, standing up, they all three followed his pointing arm to see, way up the hill, Rydd and Herbie running and looking behind them as they disappeared into the woods. "They're up to no good," said Tris.

"Maybe it's more smuggled goods up there," said Dom, for he had told Tris and Davy of his adventure on Rame.

"Let's spy on 'em," said Davy.

They ran up the rough path from the beach on to Minnadew and headed, at Tris' suggestion, over to the right of where they had seen the other three enter. There was no one in sight as they slipped up into the woods. Carefully, they crept further into the woods, towards the area where they had seen the others enter. Stealthily, they crawled up a slope over a clearing which was beneath them; they could hear voices. Ten feet below them was Rydd, proudly displaying something to Herbie, dangling it in front of his mate. Tris could see it was a gold pocket-watch. It was hidden by Herbie's body from Dom and Davy They couldn't see what it was.

"I'm goin' to sell it, and the rest, specially that jewellery box," Rydd's deep voice boasted. "We'll both be rich. But," his voice became hard and his face was grim, "you don't say a word, right? Not to anyone. Y'er in it with me – we're both in it. You don't say a word to Richie, right?" His face was close up against Herbie's.

"Course not, I won't," mumbled Herbie, his face flustered.

Despite his big frame, which was taller and wider than Rydd's, he was clearly intimidated by Rydd's strong temper.

Dom and Davy were scared of being seen and crawled back. Tris remained. Unfortunately for him, at that moment, Rydd looked up and saw Tris. His eyes flashed in surprise and anger.

Tris slithered back as fast as lightning. "Run!" he panted. They raced out of Minnadew.

He didn't see the murderous look in Rydd's eyes as he grabbed the others and clawed up the slope of the pit, shouting at them to get Tris.

They got to the lane and, looking back, saw Rydd and his mates had not yet emerged out of the woods, as it had taken them time to climb up over the pit. In a corner alleyway, out of sight from the lane, they huddled to catch their breath. They heard footsteps running down the lane. They froze. The steps pounded past and faded. They were safe, for the moment. "Rydd saw me!" explained Tris.

"Oh no!" exclaimed Davy. "They'll be after you now."

"At least they didn't see you two," replied Tris.

"What was he holding?" asked Dom.

"I'm not sure." Tris prevaricated, because he did not want them to be endangered, for Rydd had not seen Dom or Davy.

Dom swallowed. "If it is valuable, it must have been Rydd who was involved in attacking poor Mrs Grey's relative."

"He has killed a man in order to rob him," said Tris.

Davy's eyes were on stalks.

Dom spoke. "That's what my dad said; it's murder!"

"What do we do?" asked Davy in a shocked voice.

"I'm going to tell my dad; he'll know what to do. You two get home. They didn't see you in the woods and you mustn't be seen now – get home. Davy, go back over Minnadew and then back down to the shore to get to your house over the rocks; that way they won't see you." Davy nodded.

"Tris, be very careful," said Dom. "If they get you, your life won't be worth living. How are you going to get home without being seen?"

"I'll go up from here to the top road so I avoid the main street. Then I can slip down Duck Steps and it's only a few yards to my house." Duck Steps was a long flight of steps that connected the top road straight down to Garrett Street.

The three friends parted in haste. Dusk had fallen, as the sun had set at its usual winter time of late afternoon. *This would help Tris,* thought Dom as he ran into the shelter of his home.

Later after tea, a knock came at his door. It was Tris. Under cover of the dark, he had come to say his father wanted to talk to them both. Dom slipped on a jacket and they ran down Back Lane, thinking to get Davy, but they were told by his Ma that he and his dad had to go and bring back some mawn baskets from the palace. They thanked her and left, deciding it was best for just the two of them to go to the Manse. They could catch Davy up with the news tomorrow. They hurried through the deserted streets of Kingsand and, checking around the corner, they saw Garrett Street was also empty.

Once in the Manse, Pastor Kenny listened to them carefully. Tris explained again what he had seen.

Pastor Kenny considered for a moment before answering Tris.

"Since you told me earlier, I have been thinking. Rydd Bolitho may have the pocket watch and more from Mrs Grey's relative but that doesn't mean he committed the crime. It may have come into his hands from someone else. We need a clear witness."

The lads hadn't thought of that. But, as Pastor Kenny spoke the last words, Dom in a sudden flash, recalled Sol's words to him the other day. They hit him with fresh impact.

"Mr Kenny, sir," he blurted out, forgetting the Pastor's proper title. "I think – I've just remembered something! I think I might know someone who might have been a witness on that night. But I can't be sure yet."

Pastor Kenny looked troubled, "If you have the right person, we need to find out exactly what he saw – because, if you are right, Rydd, and whoever was with him, will be wanted for murder."

The word hung in the room, with impact on Dom again.

Pastor Kenny continued, "If it is them, they may have only intended to knock him down and rob him but they killed him. Poor foolish lads." He paused, "Who is it Dom? Is it someone you know well enough to talk to?" he asked.

"I – I can't say yet sir. I am sorry but I am not sure of what he saw and the person is very afraid."

Pastor Kenny looked troubled. "We will need to know. A person has died and justice must be done."

"I understand sir." Dom felt very awkward but he just didn't feel he could tell them Sol's name until he had talked to find out what Sol was so scared about.

"Will you try to see this person and find out if they are a witness?"

Dom nodded slowly. "I-I'll try," he answered.

"If he saw their identity then, once we have his word as a witness, justice can be done and I can call my friend, Mr Reynolds, the lawyer in Plymouth."

Tris saw Dom out. He was about to say something more when his father called him. Dom left in quite a state, looking to the left towards the Stephens' house where Lamorna was. The image of her being enticed by his enemy, who might even be a murderer, stung him. She was in real danger.

But I must concentrate, he told himself. He must talk to Sol.

It was late so he waited till the next morning, which was a Saturday, but Ned wanted him to clear out a shed to be ready in case they would be moving house soon, and there were logs to be chopped, which were not easy for Ned now that his best right arm had been damaged. So, despite his sense of urgency, it was late in the afternoon before he could call at Old Maudie's. She came slowly to the door, complaining about her rheumatism.

"My bones are painin," she said. "What can I do fer 'ee?"

"Is Sol around?" asked Dom, careful not to say too much.

"Ee must be down by The Cleave." She added, "He ain't been hisself: sommat's on ee's mind; he ain't been hisself for days but 'ee won't tell me," she continued. Her faded green eyes squinted at Dom like two glass beads. "There's all this trouble over the murder," she added. "I gotta feelin' it ain't finished yet." She touched his arm. "See if you can make 'im talk; he likes you."

Dom made excuses and hurried away before she could ask him something more.

Down at The Cleave the tide was out. It was drizzling. The sea was steel grey, matching his sombre mood, and a fog was advancing over the water, hiding Penlee Point completely and cloaking the Penlee woods in mystery. The air was cold and damp. Twilight was advancing. Sol was on the beach, pacing up and down by the waves. His lanky figure was hunched over with his hands in his pockets. As Dom got closer, he saw Sol's hair was uncombed and stringy with the damp. He jumped as Dom called his name.

After greeting him, Dom decided to risk it and began, "Sol, you saw somethin' bad, didn't you, the other night; the night the gentleman died? Why don't you tell me, you'll feel better if you do."

Sol looked shocked and turned away. "I-I be feared. I don't want no trouble." His voice broke into a sob. "I'm a bad man 'cos I ran away."

Dom reached up and put his arm around Sol's bony shoulder and realised his shirt was soaked. "No Sol, you're not bad, you were just afraid. You didn't do anything wrong, did you?"

"I ran away." He looked full of guilt.

"It was a shock for you – you didn't know what to do, did you?"

Sol looked a bit relieved, as if this made sense to him. "You be good, Dom. You are my friend, ain't you?" he asked anxiously. His grey eyes looked down at Dom, looking for reassurance.

"Yes, Sol, I am your friend. I won't let anyone hurt you. But you'll feel better when you tell me what you saw."

Sol gulped. "I-I saw the man on ee's horse further up on the road. I could see ee's lantern. Then, all of a sudden, real quick, someone jumped out of the hedge and pulled 'im off ee's 'orse. He fell to the ground and then there was two at 'im. I dunno where the other come from. Then they 'it 'im with a stick or somethin' – a lot they beat 'im." Sol's words were coming in a rush, as though they had been pent up and now a dam was breaking. He was speaking so fast that Dom couldn't ask the question he wanted, until Sol paused for breath.

"Sol, did you see who it was, either of them? Sol, this is important."

"I see'd sommat. I see'd a bit cos the gentleman 'ad a lantern. I see'd – I see'd the one who jumped on 'im."

"Who, Sol, who did you see?" Dom tried to keep calm.

"I – I didn't see hee's face – it was dark," Sol spluttered. His voice became a moan.

"Ee's 'orrible, 'orrible!" He bent and laid his head on Dom's shoulder and began to sob and he hugged Dom tight with a strength that Dom had never realised Sol possessed.

Dom comforted him.

"I was scared – I shoulda helped the man."

"Did anyone see you, Sol?"

"No, I was under a tree – in the dark shadow, a bit away. Will I get in trouble?" Sol's eyes were wide.

Dom's mind was racing. This was not quite the proof they needed, but it was something!

Sol asked again.

"No, no, Sol, I'll look after you. It wasn't your fault."

There was no point in telling him yet that he would have to speak to someone like Pastor Kenny, or even a lawyer.

"Come on, Sol, let's get you home in the warm; you're wet through."

As they returned back up the hill, Dom told Sol not to tell anyone – not even Maudie – until the right time. Sol nodded and promised. He was exhausted through having to tell and re-live the dark story.

After tea, Dom waited till Ned headed for the pub and then called out to Prue, who was in the kitchen, that he was going to see Tris. Before she could answer, he was gone out of the door into the darkness.

He slipped through the dark alleyways to The Manse. Pastor Kenny opened the door.

"Hello, Dom. Come in; it's a wet, dark night." Dom felt a bit uncomfortable. He had been hoping Tris would answer.

Pastor Kenny could see that Dom was tense and led him into his study.

"What's the matter?" he asked kindly, "have you discovered something?" His blue eyes searched Dom's face.

"It's – it's – well, I've talked with a witness. It was Sol."

"Oh my!" Pastor Kenny sounded disappointed.

"Sol was shocked. He kept saying 'I see'd it, I seed it' and wouldn't tell me what it was that he saw, in case it got 'im into trouble. Having talked to him, I found he was there on the night the gentleman was attacked."

"He was there? How come?"

"He was on an errand for Maudie and so was coming home from his aunt in Millbrook."

"Was he able to tell you anything?"

"Yes, sir, he saw the attack on the gentleman who was visiting Mrs Grey."

"How much did he see?"

Dom recounted the story as Sol had told it.

"So – he says there were two but he didn't actually see who either of them was?"

"No sir, but he feels bad that he was too frightened to help the old man. He's so scared sir; he's in a state."

"This is something but not enough. I need to go see Mr Grey and discuss what we do with this news."

"Yes sir, but can Sol be protected?"

"I will ensure that Dr Grey and I do not divulge Sol's name unless there comes a time when we have to. Dr Gey will want to talk with him."

"He will need to answer some questions, Dominic."

Chapter 7
A Love Lost

"The heart of man is very much like the sea; it has its storms, it has its tides and, in its depths, it has its pearls too."[7]

On the next day, which was a Sunday, it was heavy on Dom's mind to talk again to Sol but there was no opportunity because, right after breakfast, Ned required him to help with Bill Bray and the pilchard fishing. It was a long day. Ned needed Dom working with him because of having only one good arm to use, so they worked together, pulling in the catch. It wasn't as big as they'd hoped. Their hands were frozen with the cold and Dom's arms were aching. They didn't get back till evening. On their return in the twilight, they could see the lights of Pastor Kenny's church making it look like a floating lightship and the sound of hymn-singing drifted over the water. It was too late to talk privately with Sol without getting Maudie suspicious. It would have to be tomorrow.

At school the following day, the talk was still all about the murder. Several were really frightened. Lizzie Hoskins from the Ship Inn, added fuel to the story as she held court at

---

[7] Vincent Van Gogh

lunchtime, telling everyone in a loud voice that last night she overheard a customer telling her dad in the bar that Pastor Kenny had been seen visiting Dr Grey. This was unusual for Dr Grey, as a staunch Anglican would not normally have anything to do with the Pastor. Pastor and Tris always looked very healthy so he wasn't there for any illness. Perhaps, several men conjectured, he knew something about the murder? Herbie heard the girl sharing this and quizzed her hard. Who had seen this? He wanted to know. The girl was intimidated and rushed back into the classroom.

Rydd, while this was going on, had been in a corner with Herbie. They had sent Richie away on some pretext. Their heads were close together and they looked over at Tris and Dom several times. It didn't look good. After a while, they parted and then Rydd was at the far end of the yard and was again flirting with Lamorna, who seemed taken in by his easy charms and obviously admired his muscles when he bared his arm like a wrestler. He made a striking, gypsy-like figure with his dark hair and broad shoulders. Above his full lips, he was now boasting the beginnings of a moustache. The shadow of a beard was also forming from the dark stubble on his chin. He had been boasting that he would be shaving now he was sixteen, unless he chose to have a beard. He boasted that he was too old to keep on at this 'school for kids'. His virility was impressing all the girls and side-lining the boys. Even his hair had been slicked down into more order recently. After he had shown off, Herbie pulled him into a corner. After this, Rydd looked grim. Back in class, Dom, who was very aware of Rydd, noticed he was shooting many ugly glances at Tris who, as, usual, was concentrating on his work and didn't seem to notice. It didn't look good. But nothing more happened between them.

Tris slipped off at the end of school very quickly – he said he was needed to do an errand for his dad. Dom saw that Rydd had watched Tris go, his eyes sharp and thoughtful. He then sent Herbie away with some instructions which Dom could not hear. He was emphasising something strongly, with his finger jabbing at him. Herbie nodded vehemently and ran off down the lane, slipping in the mud. Rydd turned as Lamorna came past him. He became intently focused on her and drew her away from her friends, whispering he had something to show her. Dom watched from the school doorway as they both walked slowly down the hill. He followed them quietly at close quarters, increasing his own pain. They were oblivious to him. He heard her lovely laugh, again so lilting and melodic, as Rydd pulled her close. Suddenly, she clapped her hands with sudden joy and gave Rydd a warm kiss and a hug! There was a glint of gold and Rydd tenderly fastened something around her neck.

"Oh Rydd!" she gasped, "You shouldn't 'ave, it's beautiful."

"Morna," he heard Rydd's voice, husky with desire, "it's you who's beautiful."

He drew her close wrapping his arms tight around her, and then he kissed her. Dom's heart beat furiously with anguish. They walked on towards Cawsand. Rydd now had his arm boldly around her waist, holding her tight against him and she shyly put her arm around him; they walked on entwined together. Dom's heart sank. He was calling her Morna and kissing her! He turned and walked morosely home, kicking at stones. She was lost to him. Jealousy rose up like bile in his mouth. Rydd had got everything.

Despite his disappointment, before it got dark, he needed to talk with Sol. As he was going out, Prue called out for him to get a loaf, for they were out of bread. She gave him the coins. He called next door but Maudie appeared and said, "You know Sol, ee's gone down the beach to see them waves. He loves a storm."

Thanking her, Dom headed down the lane against the driving wind. The south-easter had whipped up an increasingly wild storm over the last couple of days. As he turned the sharp corner to the Cleave, the full force of it knocked him back momentarily. But, above the gulls screaming, he could hear high-pitched young voices shouting. He drew nearer to the beach to see, over in the distance, a group of young boys jumping on a tall figure. It was Sol! They were pulling his hair and yelling insults; "Dopey Sol!", "Stupid silly Solly!", "Idiyut! Idiyut! Can't beat us!"

About six of them were on him. Sol was confused and spinning around trying to throw them off; some were holding his arms. Then he lost his balance and fell on to the sand and they were on him like a pack of wolves. One of them was poking him with a stick and another whipping him with a length of seaweed. Sol was shouting incoherent cries like a wounded animal.

Dom raced forward and shouted, "Get off 'im, or I'll strap ya!"

He waded into the group and began peeling off boys with both hands. They were taken by surprise and several made a dash for it, running over the rocks towards the pilchard Palace. Dom held onto the two scruffy lads in his hands. Sol looked up with tears streaming from his eyes and scratches on his face.

"Dommy," he gasped, "Dommy!"

He looked all in. Dom was angry.

"What are your names?" he demanded, as he had not seen them before.

"Nicky," stuttered the one with ginger hair and the other began to sob in fear. "He's Dick," said Nick.

"Why did you attack him?"

"Ee came and wanted to talk to us and we realised he was a bit stupid like; not right up 'ere," he pointed to his head.

"He is not stupid – he's a friend of mine. What you're doin' is cruel and nasty," shouted Dom. "Don't you ever let me see you do this again! You say sorry to Sol – right now!" He glared at the boys.

"Sorry," they muttered, looking at Sol.

"And again," insisted Dom, "say 'sorry sir' to Sol."

They did.

"And you tell yer friends I will be after them if I see them again. Where d'you live, tell me?" he demanded fiercely.

"Over Maker way," Nick said.

"If I see you doin' anything like this again, I'll make sure yer dads know about this. Now be gone and don't come back!" He let them go and they scampered off as fast as they could go, in the direction of their friends.

Dom turned to Sol, who was still lying on his back like a landed turtle, and helped him up. He was shaken and covered in wet sand and seaweed. The gale-force wind was whipping his hair over his face. Spume, like flecks of snow, was flying over them from the breaking waves.

"Dom, thank 'ee, thank 'ee." He panted. "You saved me. You're my friend ain't you?" His troubled eyes were searching Dom's face.

Dom realised what an ordeal this had been for him. He put his arm around sodden Sol. "Yes Sol. I'll always be your friend. Those silly boys don't know what they're doin'. They're the stupid ones, not you. Come on, let's get you 'ome and warmed up."

"I won't forget," Sol stammered. "I'll 'elp you any time. I want to be there for 'ee just as you've bin 'ere for me."

"Thanks Sol, you're a good lad."

The ragged clouds flew scattered across the sky and the screaming gulls were riding the wind as if on a merry-go-round, as the two of them walked on together up Back Lane and out of the tearing wind. Sol began to calm down, reassured by Dom. Dom's errand was completely forgotten and it was not going to work to talk sense into Sol today.

The next day was after school, the wind was still strong. Finishing his jobs for Prue, Dom was determined to meet with Sol. Sure enough, it was easy to get a much-recovered Sol to join him in going to see the waves. Sol again repeated to Dom how much he had helped him.

"You'm my friend, Dom, you 'elped me an' I'll always help you."

This gave Dom the way into the conversation he needed. They had reached the Cleave and they walked to the far end, dodging the waves, and sheltered behind the wall. The afternoon light was fading under the stormy sky.

"Sol, I do need you to help me. I need you to tell me again what you saw that night up on the hill."

Sol looked scared and recounted again the events of the murder.

He ended by asking plaintively, "Am I in trouble Dom, will they take me away?"

Dom reassured him.

"Are you sure you didn't see anything more about the two who attacked the gentleman? A face or anything? Was one of them bigger than the other?"

Sol was a bit confused by three questions at once, so Dom asked them one at a time.

No, he said, he never saw a face; it was too dark. But yes, one of the attackers was bigger than the other. It was he who seemed to hit the man with a stick or something. The shorter one was bending over the body after the man was beaten and was looking for something. Then he pulled the other bigger one away and they ran into the darkness.

"Sol, you are not in trouble. You are doing really well – you are important because you saw something." Sol's eyes widened.

"Did anyone see you?"

"No, Dom. I was hid in the 'edge a bit down the 'ill."

Dom was relieved. "That's good then Sol. You're safe."

The wind was wilder and they had to talk over the sound of the surf breaking with a booming sound against the wall. It began to rain; heavy drops.

"Now, Sol, it's important that we tell someone what you saw because it could help catch these attackers before they hurt more people. Do you understand?"

Sol was uncomfortable. "I ain't no good at talkin' to folk," he said. "I gits muddled."

"I know Sol, but how would it be if I came with you and helped you?"

"Who would we have to see?"

"Tris' dad. He's a good man and kind, Sol. I'll help you."

As Dom talked on, Sol became convinced, as long as it was with Dom, and he wouldn't be in any trouble.

Dom decided to go with him right away before Sol could change his mind. In any case to wait longer would make him more tense. Together, in the growing darkness, they dodged the waves and pebbles being thrown up on the Cleave and made their way to the Manse. As Dom knocked on the door, Sol began to shake and hid behind Dom.

It was Pastor Kenny who opened the door. Dom was disappointed, he had hoped it would be Tris to start with. Pastor Kenny looked surprised to see the two of them but warmly welcomed them in and took them to his study where a gas lamp was burning, giving a welcome glow of warmth.

"Sir," said Dom, "this is Sol. He's the one I was telling you about – and he's come to talk to you about what he saw on the night of the attack."

Sol was looking down at the carpet, trembling.

The Pastor kindly said, "You are very welcome Sol – it's Solomon, isn't it?"

Sol nodded wordlessly.

"Take a seat, Sol. Any friend of Dom's is a friend of mine. Don't be afraid, Sol, we need your help; you're not in any trouble."

Sol glanced at Dom who nodded, so Sol sat down, relieved that the Pastor had reaffirmed his words.

"Just tell us what you saw, Sol; that's all we need to hear."

Haltingly, Sol, prompted now and again by Dom, told his story.

Dom explained that Sol had not seen anything more clearly to identify the two attackers. Pastor Kenny looked at Sol and asked, "Is that right?" Sol nodded several times. Pastor turned to Dom. "Dominic, I need to talk further with you but I think we could let Sol go for now. Thank you so much Sol, you have been a great help."

Sol looked relieved. Dom said, "I'll just see him out sir, and be back."

At the door Sol asked, "Is it over? What do I do now?"

Now was not the time to tell him that he may have to see a lawyer and tell his story again.

"Yes, it's over for now. You did fine." He patted him on the back. "Now Sol, go home but mind you don't say anything to anyone, not even Maudie. Can you keep this a secret? Will you promise?"

Sol nodded vehemently, "I promise."

Dom said, "I'll see you tomorrow."

He slipped out into the night and Dom returned to the study.

"Well done, Dom," said Pastor. "It is something, but it is not enough to convict anyone. I have been to Dr Grey and told him about the possible witness; now I will need to go and tell him about this."

"Yes sir, I'm sorry it couldn't be more." He paused. "Is Tris around?"

"No, I can't understand it. He should have been back by now from Maker. Perhaps he stayed for a cup of tea and a bite. He said he might call on you if it wasn't too late."

"I'd best go home and see if he is there," said Dom, getting up.

"You're a good lad, Dom. Well done for bringing Sol here. He obviously trusts you."

Dom was unused to being praised and blushed bright red.

"Thank you, sir," he said huskily.

He raced home but only Prue was there and told him no one had called.

That evening he waited but reckoned that Tris must have been so late he had gone straight home. The storm raged outside, rain drummed against the windows, the wind whistled and moaned around the house and blew so hard under the door that they packed a rug against the gap. Prue threw more logs on the fire.

Chapter 8
Grief

"To weep is to make less the depth of grief." [8]

Dom awoke early from a restless night with a sense of foreboding that he couldn't shake off. He felt an urgency to meet Tris and hear his news. He ran down to The Manse through deserted streets and knocked on the door. Pastor Kenny answered immediately and looked dishevelled and strained.

"Is Tris home now?" asked Dom.

The answer was not what he expected.

"No, Dom. He did not come home last night. I have sent a message at dawn this morning to my friends, who he was visiting. I am hoping that he stayed the night, because it was so foul. But it is unlike him. I am waiting for their reply."

At that very moment a young lad ran from the street down the short alley to the door with a note in his hand. The Pastor gave him a coin and hurriedly opened the note. His face lost all its colour.

---

[8] William Shakespeare

"O my Lord, they never saw Tris. He didn't even get to them last night!"

Fear gripped Dom's heart. "We must look for him – maybe he had an accident. I will get Davy."

"Yes, yes. I will alert a search party."

With that, Dom started straight away. His heart was hammering like a drum as he ran back into Kingsand. He quickly called Davy, who was as shocked by the news as he was.

"Where was he going last night?" asked Davy.

"Over to Pastor's church members who live at the bottom of Maker hill right near the shore. He'd have gone over the rocks here as a short cut."

They started out towards the Palace over the pinkish rocks with their many rock pools and crevices. They had to avoid slipping on the wet seaweed which covered so many of the rocks.

The morning was still rough with the wind driving torn clouds across the sky. The sea, grey as iron, under the dark clouds, was still wild, with waves topped by many white horses across the bay. The tide was on the turn and, in a few hours, would reveal the beach again.

Dom got out his telescope and searched; nothing but water and rocks. As they were passing the King's Way path opening, Davy, his tangled dark hair blowing all over the place, asked, "Should we also search Minnadew?"

"Not yet. Pastor said Tris would take the short route over these rocks. We could search up there later. He may have chosen to return that way in the dark."

The lads pressed on, with the wind rocking them off balance as they jumped over the rocks.

There was no sign of anything. Suddenly they heard snatches of voices in the distance behind them, coming in broken sounds on the wind. They looked back. There was a small group of men starting out from the village. The search party was under way. More noises came from up above them on Minnadew, as men shouted Tris' name.

Davy voiced the fear that was haunting Dom. "D'you think somethin' bad 'appened to Tris?"

"Davy, it's not looking good. I am hoping against hope."

After another few minutes they were on the shingle tossed up against the Palace walls. It was deserted, as it was too early for workers yet.

They pressed on. Dom scanned again with his 'scope; and then he spotted it. He grabbed Davy's arm and pointed. Bobbing on the water was a red cap.

"It's Tris' cap!" His cap was a distinctive leather cap of good quality. Dom had always admired it. Dom felt a sick dread grip his stomach.

They ran towards the sea's edge and there, caught in a cleft in the rocks was the sight they had hoped never to see. The body was face down and moving with the swell of the waves. Weirdly, and cruelly, it jerked as though still alive.

"O God, no! Please don't let it be! Tris!" screamed Dom jumping into the water. Davy, not normally very vocal, shouted "No! Oh no Tris!"

Together, they caught hold of the sodden body and turned it over in the water.

The blonde hair was partly covering his dear face. A harsh gash was across his scalp and another on the neck. The face was bruised and battered by the rocks and waves.

Both sobbing, they hauled the body, with difficulty because of the sodden clothes, on to the rocks. Water streamed from his mouth and clothes. Dom threw himself over his friend, hugging him. and sobbing. "O Tris, Tris, my dear friend! Who did this to you? You can't leave us like this; it can't be true. Why, why o why? Why you and not us?" They did not know that Tris had been in greater danger because he had seen the gold pocket watch. He had kept it from them. Davy stood, in shock, with tears streaming down his face; his lips were moving but no sound would come.

Davy came to himself and said, "I'll go get Pastor Kenny and the men." He ran off across the rocks towards Girt Beach. Another sharp arrow went through Dom's already battered heart. Pastor Kenny! Tris' father! Now he had lost his dear and only son, as well as his wife.

Dom held his friend against him in unbelief. The head fell on his chest and he cradled him as the grief increased. His closest friend, the truly good, caring Tris; come to this. Desperately, he wished for a miracle, to see him breathe again. But nothing.

The rest of that day, and the days following, became a tear-stained blur of misery. Dom would never forget Pastor Kenny and others drawing near and the father's heart-rending grief as he lifted the body of his son from Dom up into his arms and wept over him.

In the days following, both villages were in a state of shock. Maudie called with Sol at the Martyns' house and spoke to Dom.

"I'm so sorry for 'ee and the pastor. I told 'ee death was comin'." She paused and her eyes gleamed. "And, Dom, it ain't over yet. The sea has more to claim. You mark my words; the guilty will be punished." Dom couldn't understand her words. Sol hugged Dom again and again; Dom was surprised at his strength. Dom wanted Maudie to say more but her lips tightened, her eyes narrowed and she turned away, tightening her shawl around her thin body, and muttering to herself.

After the terrible shock, Pastor Kenny had mourned his son but bore his grief with fortitude. His small congregation rallied around, preparing meals and offering help in warm-hearted sympathy. Tris had been popular and, because many pupils were upset, the decision was taken to close the school early for Christmas. Door-to-door questioning took place, led by Pastor, Dr Grey and Mr Trevelyan. Nothing was forthcoming. Everyone had been at home except for those who had been in the pub. It had been such a wild stormy night. All claimed to have witnesses who were with them. No one had seen anything. If they had, they weren't saying.

"What we need is a police force, like they have started in Newcastle," said the doctor grimly. The main question was whether the gash was caused by a fall from the rocks or by an attacker. The story most favoured was an accident. Dom and Davy were not at all convinced. First the gentleman and now Tris. Could it have been Rydd and his gang – but why? Why Tris and not them? Was it because Rydd had spotted him that day in the woods? Dom's mind whirled around and around the issue without any clearer understanding. The grief of missing his closest friend intensified. Prue tried to comfort him by cooking his favourite dishes and a lardy cake but he had no appetite. Even Ned said how sorry he was.

There was much sympathy for the Pastor in his loss. Hearts that had been hardened against his religion, which they had not understood, were softened now in many folks by common sympathy for a loving father's loss; this they did understand. Even Mr Trevelyan sent a message of condolence. Both villages were more united for once, in a common emotion.

A few days later, the small chapel was packed, as never before. Dom had never been to any such church. He was struck by how very plain the interior was, with no pictures or statues. With a lot of passion, the congregation sang hymns Dom did not know. Pastor Kenny bravely stood at the pulpit and spoke movingly of his dear son. People wept. Dom could not comprehend how the Pastor could go on believing in a God that would allow such a tragedy to his son. One thing he said struck Dom. "My God knows my grief, for his only son also died."

Afterwards, the walking funeral took place. It was a biting cold but dry December morning, a few days before Christmas. Dom was used to seeing this sort of funeral in the village, but he had never been personally affected before, nor felt such loss and pain. He walked behind Pastor Kenny who was bareheaded.

In the days after the tragedy Dom had felt to call on the Pastor and had been welcomed with a big hug. This caused a fresh dam to break in Dom and the tears came, as the Pastor held him. Tears were in the older man's eyes too, as they sat down.

"I am in pain over my dear son, as you are. He had such promise and was such a good son."

Dom nodded sadly. "Tris was my very best friend." His voice choked as the tears welled up again.

"Tristan was fond of you, Dom. He always spoke of you with affection."

"Sir, have you found out anythin' about this terrible thing?"

"No, Dom. We have questioned everyone and uncovered nothing."

"What about the Bolithos? Or their mates, the Stephens or Dick Grills?"

"They all have witnesses or say they were either at home that evening or in the pub. Why do you ask about them specifically? Is it the smuggling connection?"

"Yes sir, but it is especially about Rydd Bolitho. Sir, I'm sure the Bolithos were involved. I believe Rydd may well have been the one poor Sol saw in the robbery of Mrs Grey's relative. Also, Rydd hated Tris. I think he was jealous of his abilities but also afraid of him, more than of Davy and me, for some reason."

"Why?"

"Tris was always the strong and confident one of us three and Rydd knew he couldn't bully Tris like he could me or Davy. But I also wonder if Tris saw something up in the woods once, when we spied on Rydd and Herbie Wilcox. They saw Tris but never saw us and we all made our escape."

"The Bolithos have always been a rough lot but, Dom, without proof, we must not spread suspicion. All are equal in God's sight – and in God's eyes, and the law, all are innocent until proved guilty. Nothing can be proved through Sol's words."

"But sir, don't you want revenge for Tris? He was strong and wouldn't have died from an accidental fall. He was a good swimmer, too. I believe he was killed." Dom's voice broke,

"I hate Rydd and his gang and family." Anger flared up in him as he spoke.

Pastor Kenny put his arm on Dom's. "Dom, there is much I do not know. But I do know what the Bible says is true." He turned to the large Bible on his desk and, opening it, said "Romans 12 verse 19 says this: 'Vengeance is mine, I will repay, saith the Lord'. God is saying that any vengeance is best left in his hands. This means that only God knows what happened and he will judge those who were involved; if it was as you say. Revenge will only cause your heart to become bitter and hard. Whoever killed my Tristan has robbed me of my only son. I have to live with that pain and loss but, if someone murdered him, they will have to live with their guilt. And they will have a dark future. My Tristan is in heaven with his mother and I will see him again. Any murderer is heading for hell; a future forever separated from God. If they repent, they can be forgiven, Dom, even for such a terrible deed. As a Christian I am required to forgive all sinful acts against me or my son as I have been forgiven through Jesus Christ."

Dom's eyes were wide in surprise at the Pastor's words. *Forgiveness? For the likes of Bruiser and his kind? And Pastor's comment that he would see Tris again was spoken with a really firm hope and conviction. Tris? In heaven?* He could see Pastor firmly believed what he said. *Could it be true? Ned always said that death is the end; that there was nothing else. Was there really a God, a God who judges? A heaven and a hell?*

"I dunno," Dom answered, a bit embarrassed and feeling out of his depth.

Pastor Kenny, seeing Dom's confusion, changed the subject.

"Would you and Davy, as Tris' closest friends, walk with me behind the coffin after the funeral service?" he asked. "My few relatives are living far up north and will not come."

Dom was touched. Pastor explained that, because there was no room for a burial ground near the chapel, they would be burying Tristan up at Maker church.

But when the pastor asked him if he would say a prayer of thanksgiving for Tris at the graveside burial, Dom clammed up. He wouldn't know what to say in front of people and he had never prayed.

He looked so awkward that the pastor said, "I understand. But would you and Davy just walk with me?"

"Yes sir, we will." It was the least he could do.

Rumours and gossip swept the communities. Two deaths so quick in succession! One was definitely murder, and no one had been caught. Regarding Tris, some said he must have fallen and got into difficulties coming over the dark rocks in such a stormy night.

"Could it be suicide?" some asked who had never known Tris.

The day of the funeral passed in a blur. Dom and Davy walked together with Pastor behind the coffin. Dom couldn't bear to look at it or think of his friend imprisoned in it. He walked with his head bowed. As they trudged through the streets, all he could think of were the images of Tris which kept passing through his mind. The adventures they'd had; his friend's laugh, his handsome face, their swimming and exploring Rame together. His heart was weighing him down, with a lead weight. On the brief occasion he did look up, he saw that the narrow streets were lined with people, dressed in black out of respect.

Some were saying, "God bless 'ee, Pastor."

Some women were weeping. Flowers were thrown on to the coffin. There were many pupils who had liked Tris. At one point, he saw Bruiser who was a head and shoulders over others, with Connie on one side of him and Sid on the other. He hadn't wanted to see them so looked away quickly without seeing their expressions. In front of her father was Lamorna. His eyes met hers and lingered. She smiled sadly through her tears at them and threw a flower. *Was it to Pastor or to him that she smiled,* wondered Dom? There was no sign of Rydd or his cronies.

They reached the edge of the village and there the coffin was laid on a wagon and pulled slowly up the long hill to Maker with just a few following; mostly from the chapel. There, on the top of the hill, in a cutting wind, Tristan Kenny, was laid to rest. Pastor Kenny recited some Bible verses and gave thanks as he committed his son to God. In the pause that followed, Dom found that, to his surprise, he did want to speak some words to his friend.

He blurted out, "Thank you Tris. You were my wonderful friend. I'll never forget you." And, he added quickly, "Thank you God for 'im."

After this he looked uncertainly at the pastor, in case he was out of order. But the pastor's kind eyes met his and were smiling. He nodded his head to Dom in thanks. And so, the coffin was lowered into the grave.

Dom could not bear any more and stepped away from it with Davy. It was too final. His friend was truly gone.

The pastor came across to them as earth was being thrown into the grave and said: "Thank you lads and thank you, Dom. That was a special prayer." He continued, "You lads are always welcome at my house. Come and play the board games sometimes. My home will seem empty now."

People were waiting to gather around him so he turned back to speak with them.

The two lads walked sombrely back down the hill together; hardly a word was spoken. Each was full of his own thoughts. *It's over,* thought Dom, *but life will never be the same.*

Chapter 9
A Fresh Start?

Countless as the sands of the sea are human passions.[9]

That Christmas was the worst ever. Gloom and grief hung, as palpable as a shroud, over the village, matched by the dark, cold, winter days. Prue tried her best to cheer Dom up by cooking a fine lardy cake but he had little appetite.

The new year of 1821 dawned with a brighter day of sunshine, which at least made the cold weather seem better. There also came the brighter news that the coastguard cottage on Penlee was ready for Ned to live in and start work. Ned lost no time in swiftly arranging for their few possessions and bits of furniture to be loaded on his mate's large wagon. Sol helped them load it. He kept saying, "I'll miss 'ee, Dom. I'll miss 'ee." After everything was loaded, he surprised Dom by giving him a strong, bony hug that nearly forced the breath out of his body.

"Sol, you're always welcome over at our house. I'm your friend," Dom reassured him, as he caught his breath.

---

[9] Nikolai Gogol

Sol nodded gratefully, with a tear in his eye. Old Maudie also nodded approvingly at his words and hugged Prue.

She couldn't resist a word of warning: "I know you needed the job Ned, but take care. There could be trouble." She added with emphasis, "I see flames."

Dom and Prue were shocked, but Ned simply said goodbye gruffly and ignored her as he got up on the wagon with them. So, as the horse pulled them up the winding lane, they took leave of both their cottage which had been home for many years and also of Kingsand village.

Ned had planned that they would take the high road around the top of the villages rather than going through Cawsand, where he knew they'd face antagonism from the village, and especially from the smuggling community. In an hour they arrived at their new home. It was not much bigger than their previous home but in a superior position. It was in the shelter of Penlee woods but, from the back, it looked out over the bay. The garden ran down to the low cliff just 50 yards up from the sea and the rocks below. Prue was excited and ran into the house to explore the rooms. Ned and Dom began to unload the furniture.

The cottage was damp but a fire quickly made it warmer and more welcoming. Ned and Dom worked hard at carrying beds, bedding, clothes and some other bits and pieces of furniture in and upstairs. Prue busied herself, singing happily, arranging the room and unpacking their small amount of china, kitchen utensils and curtains. She soon made the main room look homely.

Later, they all three went out into the gently sloping garden and took in the view.

"Oh, it's lovely," exclaimed Prue, clapping her hands, "lovely to 'ave a view after Back Lane where all we could see was the cottages opposite. Here there's light and space."

Even Ned looked a bit brighter. "We'll get diggin' and plantin' in the Spring; it'll save us money." He turned and left them.

Prue said, "O Dom, I feel we will be happy here."

"I hope so," he answered, but inside he couldn't shake off the grief of losing his best friend. This was the first of many new things that he would now never be able to share with his friend.

Prue gave him a hug, "I must go hang the curtains," she said and went in singing again.

Dom stood looking out over the wide bay of Plymouth Sound. He could see the breakwater in the centre with some boats around it; it looked foreshortened from this angle but he had heard it was a mile long. Over beyond it was Jennycliffe in the far distance. Turning to his left there was a completely different perspective of the two villages from this viewpoint. They looked like one long village. He could see the chapel jutting out like the prow of a boat. As he did so, pain gripped him again, at the loss of his friend and at the thought of Pastor Kenny and what he must be feeling. *Was Tris really in a place called heaven?* He sighed. If, as he suspected, it was the Bolithos' doing, would they ever be brought to justice? *At least, he thought, at least we are free of the Bolithos. This is a fresh start.* He was not to know how wrong he was.

Opposite them was Kingsand and Maker hill looming above it. Then beyond, stretched the earl of Edgecumbe's estate with its densely wooded hills and, in the distance, partly hidden around the headland, was the less distinct shape of

Plymouth town and harbour. His eye scanned nearer towards the Palace on the rocks. He quickly turned away as the memory of Tris, floating by those rocks, pierced him with pain again.

He turned to look again at Cawsand and thought of Lamorna. He thought again of how he had seen her in the funeral crowd, looking sympathetic and tearful, standing in front of her dad, Sid. *Surely, he knew something?* Prue, standing opposite them, had looked longer at Bruiser, Sid and Connie. Sid's face was an expressionless mask, she said, but Bruiser's was hard. Connie just looked sad. *Lamorna! If only she wasn't so deceived by Rydd!* He supposed school would start again soon. *How would it be without Tris? How could he possibly be in the same room with Rydd?* At that moment Prue called him to come and help. He turned from his thoughts and went indoors.

The days passed as they settled in. Ned seemed happier, although his arm and shoulder clearly pained him at times. Dom had to take more of the heavy jobs, collecting logs and branches daily from the woods and starting to dig up the garden wherever it wasn't too frozen by the shade. Ned's work now involved staying awake at night to watch the bay and to check as far as Penlee Point, which was just a quarter of an hour's fast walking away. So began a new routine of Ned sleeping part of the day, which left them freer, although they had to keep quiet so as not to disturb him. Dom was now so much nearer to Rame that he couldn't wait for an opportunity to get there again.

Prue was relieved that now, at last, she didn't have to worry quite so much about Ned's loss of income from the fishing. On her first shopping day she decided to shop in

Cawsand. It was nearer and would mean not carrying heavy bags all the way from Kingsand. Also, she could fit in a visit to Aunt Lettie. She walked the mile or so through the woods and descended the lane into the village square. At its centre stood the village pump with some women around it. One of the women spotted her, and obviously alerted the others, for they turned and watched her. Most were wearing workday turbans, which emphasised their hard faces. She was about to greet them but there was no greeting on their faces; their eyes were sharp and their mouths hard.

She entered the shop. There was a woman in front of her making her purchases. The shop was run by Pete and Polly Pascoe. Large Polly, with her big apron straining over her ample bosom and waist, was weighing out some vegetables on the scales. Polly was a friend of Aunt Lettie and, although surprised to see Prue in her shop, she gave a brief smile of greeting whilst concentrating on her scales. The woman in front of Prue turned as Polly had looked up. It was Bruiser's wife, Connie, who was half the size of her husband, with a pinched face and straggling hair.

"What are you doin' 'ere?" Her eyes narrowed and she jabbed a finger at Prue. "You're no part of us. Your pa is a traitor, joinin' the Searchers." She spat the last words out and turned away, stuffing her purchases in her bag.

Prue was stunned at the wave of ferocity. She didn't know what to say. Polly spoke up quickly.

"Connie, that's no way to speak to a customer in my shop." Connie scowled, and throwing her money down, pushed past Prue, knocking her off balance, and stalked out of the shop. Prue was shaken.

"Don't 'ee worry Prue, it's the first time you've come. Connie has a mean temper on her fer such a skinny lady. They say Bruiser hits her about, 'specially when 'ee's in drink."

"I don't know, Polly, perhaps I was silly to come but it's so much nearer now."

"I know. But there's strong feelin' in this village about yer dad joinin' the coastguard watch. I know yer dad's accident is a problem and 'ee needs work. You be welcome in my shop and Pete will say the same. We can't afford to refuse any customer either – times are hard."

Prue thanked her. Polly continued, "P'raps it'd be better if you came around dinnertime to shop, say between twelve and one? It's always quieter then; there'll be less folk around 'ere as most be cookin' the midday meal for their fellas."

"Maybe," replied Prue sadly.

"In time it may well die down – so don't 'ee worry." She added kindly.

As Prue left with her purchases, she was worried; she felt like an outcast, despite Polly's kindness. Avoiding looking at the village pump, she turned quickly up the lane from the square to visit Aunt Lettie. As she left the square, she heard the word 'scum' shouted at her.

"It hurt," she told Aunt Lettie, with tears in her eyes. Her aunt comforted her with a hug.

Aunt Lettie was a widow in her seventies. Her Tom had passed away years before. Her kind old eyes were fading but she kept herself trim and her hair, as always, was firmly tied back in a bun under her lace cap.

"This is a mean village, my girl." She echoed Polly's words. "I'm truly sorry for 'ee. The Bolithos rule the roost 'ere and the Stephens and the Gills are in their pockets. I'd've preferred to be in Kingsand but Tom needed the work 'ere and Dick Grills let us 'ave this cottage at small rent because Tom was a good reliable worker in the fishin'. But as you know, my Tom would have nothin' to do with any smugglin'."

After more chat over a cup of tea and a bun about the new home, Prue took her leave and made her way home. She was still upset about the rough encounter she'd had. Her friend, Susie Hancock, had warned her. She was right. She had told her their name was dirt in Cawsand and some felt the same in Kingsand.

"They're sayin' you be traitors cos yer dad's gone over to the other side by helpin' the Searchers. But I understands yer needs."

What should she do? Prue wondered, as she remembered all these words.

She unburdened herself to Dom. He gave her a big hug and sympathy.

"I wish I'd been with you, Prue. At least Polly accepted you; I guess we just have to let the village feelins' die down."

Two nights later it was obvious the feelings weren't dying down. They were in their beds when there was a sudden crash of splintering glass. Jumping up, they headed down the stairs. Through the half open door to the living room there was a strange light flickering. All three rushed in to find the front window had a gaping hole and fire from a tree branch was lighting up the room and scorching the rug. Prue screamed. Ned grabbed the end of the branch and threw it straight out through the hole again. There, amongst the jagged pieces of glass on the rug, was a large stone and a rough paper around it. Dom picked it up and, unwrapping it, he read aloud, "Scum

– get out before we chase you out." Prue began to tremble and shake. Dom comforted her.

"They hate us Dom," she said through her tears, "they hate us."

Ned was furious and rushed outside but it was pitch black and there was no sign of anyone. Prue was still shaking and Dom swept up the glass. The room was cold with the night air pouring in.

"Blasted people!" shouted Ned as he came back in. "I'll catch 'em one night – and make 'em pay – see if I don't." He got a piece of wood from the back garden and nailed it to cover the hole.

Dom had thought they would be safe here. *What would happen next?* He wondered, as they went back to bed.

It was soon to be Spring. School was to open and Dom thought longingly about Lamorna. At least, she wouldn't be with Rydd every day, now he was at work with Bruiser. Ned had instructed Dom to take off school and to stay around for a few days so that Prue, who was still shaken by the events, had some company. After Ned had caught up on some sleep following his night-watch, his duties included him going searching the coastland during the day for signs of hidden contraband.

As Prue recovered, she was happy for Dom to be out, as long as he was within shouting distance should she need him. The nearby woods were a great solace to Dom as he roamed around them. Ned had still kept him off school after the brick incident for several weeks. As well as giving him many jobs, gardening and getting plenty of fuel for the fire, Ned knew that Dom liked exploring the coast around Penlee Point and Rame. So, after some weeks had passed without further incident, Ned told him to keep close watch wherever he went, to see if there was anything suspicious around the coves or any dubious activity on the boats. He gave Dom the markings of some of the Cawsand boats especially.

As life returned to normal without any more attacks, Dom could get around Penlee Point and over to Rame much more quickly, now they were nearer. It only took him half the time it had taken from Kingsand. It was a constant joy to be there, watching the wild wheeling of the sea birds through his telescope and being energised by the bracing air, open sky and sea. With his trusty 'scope he also delighted in scanning the bay to get a close look at the boats sailing in and out to Plymouth Sound. It was the wide horizon that fascinated him. With the 'scope's aid he could examine Smeaton's lighthouse which was about seven miles out, sticking up like a little finger above the horizon. Sometimes he could even make out one of the keepers meeting a boat with their provisions. *One day,* he thought, *when he was older, he would sail out across that wide expanse of water and explore, even as far as France.*

It was always daytime when he was at Rame. Despite keeping a watch, on Ned's orders, he had not seen any signs of smuggling. It was common knowledge in the villages that Bruiser and his gang had used their own beach under cover of darkness, where they unloaded speedily and hid the contraband, firstly under their fishing nets, but then moved the goods up to the cellars in trusted houses above the Square. They also used secret tunnels, unknown to the Searchers, to store the kegs and other desirable things until they could be distributed to the wealthy.

Dom and Davy had got together a few times, but Davy's dad had also taken him also out of school now to work full-time on the fishing boats as he had lost some workers to illness. Dom was partly relieved to be out of school a while, but it also meant he didn't see so much of Lamorna. When would she discover the truth about Rydd?

Meanwhile, when he could, he found solace in the happy hours spent in the woods around their home, spotting birds and sometimes tracking a deer up in the higher woods. It was one such day he had the joy of stalking a fine deer right up on the top ridge. He had kept his distance and the wind was in his favour. He admired the size of it and its sensitive head with antlers beginning to grow on it, turning to listen. After watching him through his 'scope, he was feeling hungry and so he started back down the hill though the dense woods.

Suddenly, he heard raised voices lower down the hill. He headed towards them. As he got nearer, he recognised a female voice crying and sobbing. It was answered by the voice Dom knew only too well. Rydd was angry. Dom got stealthily close enough to see them, below him in a dell.

"How d'you know?" Rydd snarled. *That snaking voice again,* thought Dom.

"I haven't had my time of the month for two months now. I think I'm expecting a baby – I think I'm pregnant!" she cried.

Dom caught his breath in shock.

"It's not mine!" Rydd shouted, "You bitch – you bin cheatin' on me!"

"How can you say that?" she cried with distress in her voice. "I've never been with anyone but you."

"It's nothin' to do with me!" he shouted.

"It is," she pleaded, "you know it's yours. You forced me that New Year's Eve. I never wanted to – you made me." With that, Rydd raised his arm and struck her across the face. As she fell down with a cry amongst the leaves, he jumped on her, punching her.

Anger flared in Dom and galvanised him into action. He charged at Rydd shouting, "You bully – stop 'ittin' her!"

Rydd got up in surprise and was caught off his guard. Dom aimed straight for Rydd's face. His right fist connected with his fleshy nose and blood spurted out.

Then, before Rydd could do anything else, Dom went in with his left fist, as Tris had taught him, straight into Rydd's stomach. It was just as Rydd had once done to him, long ago.

Rydd was winded. Lamorna screamed and cowered amongst the beech leaves in the dell.

"You bastard!" shouted Rydd, bending over in pain, as rich red blood streamed down over his shirt. "You bastard," he panted again.

Dom was feeling released; energy was flowing through him. He landed another blow and another at the bully. "Leave her alone," he panted, "you leave her alone. Get away from her."

Rydd, like all bullies, was a coward without his henchman to back him. He turned suddenly and stumbled down the hill. At the bottom he turned.

"I'll get you!" he yelled, "You bloody pig. You see if I don't. You and your dad are scum, filthy scum."

"You're the scum!" shouted Dom. "I've heard what you did to her an' if you ever bother her again, I'll make sure everyone knows!" Rydd turned and ran off as fast as his legs could carry him.

Dom turned to Lamorna. She lay amongst the leaves, stunned and tearful. But she was looking at Dom with new eyes. He stood breathless but exhilarated, even though his knuckles were bruised and bloody.

He knelt down beside her.

"Ee's horrible, so horrible, Dom," she sobbed, "He f-forced hisself on me. Then he threatened me he'd do me in, if I ever told. He said if I ever left 'im, I was done for."

Dom, touched by her grief, put his arm around her without thinking, and drew her to himself. She yielded. He felt at last he had proved himself and here, in his arms, was the girl of his dreams. Her blonde hair was dishevelled; her face was tear-stained and there was a red weal across her cheek; but she was still beautiful.

"Are you hurt?" he asked tenderly.

"I'm a bit sore but, oh Dom, thank you, thank you so much. You saved me."

"As long as you're alright," he held her close; she was shaking. He felt strong.

"But, Oh Dom, I'm sure I'm pregnant; I've been getting' mornin' sickness. I'm so ashamed. I can't tell me dad; he'll throw me out. He's always threatened with that if I got into trouble. I don't know what to do. I'm only just fifteen."

"Hush," he whispered, "we'll help you." He had no idea exactly how, but he felt sure something would work out. This felt so good!

As they talked together, he told her how he'd always loved her since the first day of school. She was amazed. "But I was afraid of Rydd," he continued, "and I thought you loved him."

"Well, I did, at first," she admitted, "cos he was so 'andsome and charmin'. But once he forced himself on me that New Year's Eve," she shuddered at the memory, "everythin' changed. I was afraid of 'im; he was so strong. But you were marvellous today, so brave."

Her words were music to his ears.

"Come back to our house for a bit," he said. "My sister Prue will help you. She'll know what to do."

He helped her up and, still holding her hand, he led her down out of the woods, feeling the proudest young man in the world.

Fortunately, Prue was at home baking and Ned was out working. As they came in the door, she was surprised, but with one look at her appearance she quickly realised Lamorna was in need of comfort.

"Whatever's happened, dear?" she asked, taking her by the hand and sitting her down.

Lamorna was embarrassed, but encouraged by Prue's kindness, told her the whole story again and how her father would disown her.

"I'm so ashamed," she said again and again, her face flushed bright pink.

"From what you're sayin' it's not your fault at all." Prue patted her arm. "You ain't the first and you won't be the last to be taken in by a bad 'un."

"Whatever do I do?" Lamorna's trusting eyes were fixed on Prue.

"Do any of your friends know about this?"

Lamorna shook her head. "No, I wasn't able to trust anyone, in case it got back to me dad."

"'Ere's my advice, dearie. For now, you won't be showin' anythin, for another month or so. Just let's wait and think what's best to do. Try to carry on as normal."

This made sense to Lamorna and she calmed down and agreed to Prue's advice. She was not to say anything to anyone. It was almost certain that Rydd wouldn't either, after what Dom had threatened.

Prue smiled as she said, with a twinkle in her eye, "It looks to me as if someone else around 'ere wants to take care of you." She grinned at Dom, who beamed. "So," she continued, "you're welcome 'ere anytime. We'll stand with you. We are your friends."

With profuse thanks, Lamorna hugged her and then Dom, who said, "Meet me here whenever you can get away." He thought quickly: "I have an idea; I've been thinkin'. I have a telescope and, if you go to the end of Garrett Street, overlooking the beach, when no one's around at, say, four in the afternoon, after school; I'll be looking from 'ere in the garden. If you wave, it'll mean you're comin' over and I'll be sure to meet you in the woods halfway. If you can't come that day, shake your head; I'll see it with the 'scope. If you are in trouble, cross your arms across your chest and I'll come to the edge of the village where the woods end and meet you there."

Lamorna agreed. This gave her security. He walked her part-way back through the woods. She hugged him again and left. As she left the woods, she looked back and waved.

As he entered the house again, filled with hope, Prue said, "Well, Dom, it seems obvious to me what we must do. The poor girl's in a fix and not one of her own making. We must take her in before she shows she's expectin'."

Dom breathed a sigh of mixed relief and pure pleasure. It would keep her safe and, best of all, she would be with him all the time.

"Prue, that's great. But, what about Dad?"

"Leave it to me, to win yer dad over. It may take time," she warned. "But, for all his moods, yer Dad will 'elp anyone in real trouble, especially when it's someone sufferin' from Sid Stephens or the Bolithos."

Dom went to bed that night a very happy young man; he was happier and more at peace than he ever remembered in his whole life. His mind was full of the memory of holding Lamorna for the first time and how she nestled into him. Defeating Rydd was a bonus on top of everything. Life was good!

Little did he know.

Chapter 10
A Plague?

"Roll on deep and dark blue ocean, roll."[10]

The Spring weather was warming up. Ned hadn't said any more about going back to school, which surprised Dom. Although it would have meant seeing Lamorna, he didn't miss the school or the work; so he kept quiet. To Dom's surprise, Sol turned up a number of times. Often, he just appeared like a ghost from behind some trees. "I miss 'ee, Dom," he said. "It is alright fer me to come ain't it?" he asked plaintively.

"Course it is, Sol, you're my friend. I'm glad fer you to come, particular as it's a long walk from Kingsand."

Sol looked relieved. When he came, he didn't have much to say, although, at first, he was worried about having to tell what he saw on the night of the robbery. Dom reassured him that nothing more was needed. They would walk together around Penlee, where they could go swimming from the rocks. Dom was impressed again at how long Sol could stay under water after diving. He truly was different in the water. Out of it he was gangly and awkward and shy. In it, he was

---

[10] Lord Byron

coordinated and fearless. On some occasions, Dom even shared Rame, leading Sol along the undulating rough path along the cliff. Sol liked it there; especially when Dom let him use his telescope.

"It's magic," he exclaimed many times, as he spied the fishing boats far out.

Since the death of Tris, Dom had visited the Manse several times. He had felt so sad for Pastor Kenny and the pastor seemed to really understand Dom's grief. Talking it out helped them both. He grew more and more impressed by the older man's kindness to him; his understanding and his unshakeable trust in his God, despite his own huge loss. He clearly did believe that Tris was in heaven and he would see him again one day. This gave him a comfort that Dom did not have. There seemed no light on the whole incident, although Dom was convinced that the Bolithos, and especially Rydd, must be at the bottom of it. He felt angry and helpless.

"How can they get away with it?" he said passionately to the pastor one night. "First the old man and now Tris, both gone." He avoided using the awful word 'dead'. "Couldn't you talk to the Bolithos?"

Even as he said it, he could imagine that Pastor Kenny would be beaten up if he did.

Pastor Kenny replied calmly, "I feel just as badly as you do, Dom, at this injustice but as Dr Grey and I have talked, we agree that, without clear proof, we can't get anywhere. We have to leave it to God."

This didn't make a lot of sense to Dom. *If there was a God, why had he let this happen to Tris and why wasn't there some proof?*

One evening as they played draughts together, the pastor looked Dom in the eye and said gently, "Dom, I hope you won't misunderstand me, but I feel a real affection for you, almost as though you were a son." He added, "Not that I want to draw you away from your own dad."

Dom was so deeply touched and warmed by the words of acceptance and value that his eyes filled up and he replied huskily, "Thank you, Pastor. My dad has never shown any love to me. I think it's because I caused my ma's death. He blames me for his loss." He continued to tell the pastor the whole story about his birth.

"Dom, it was never your fault," explained the pastor gently. "You were a baby. It is just one of the sad things that can happen. I'm sorry you have taken the blame but believe me, you are not to blame. It is the bitterness of grief, even as we feel it now, that has affected your father. Poor man."

Dom felt as though a load had lifted from his heart at the pastor's words. As he left that night, he thanked him again and impulsively gave him a big hug, which the older man returned.

Ned told Dom he wasn't going back to school. "I bin thinkin'," he said, one evening in a rare talkative mood. "You've done enough school – and anyway, they'm talkin' about us payin' somethin' towards it these days. I think we and the Searchers might be able to use your sharp eyes and your telescope. You could be a look-out around the coast and maybe, in time, there might be some cash, if you prove yerself." For once in his life, Dom could warm to what his dad was proposing – and he could agree with him wholeheartedly. Ned looked pleased.

During that Spring, Dom and Lamorna spent good times together getting to know each other. Right from the start, she wanted to explain more about how she had been taken in by Rydd's deceptive charm.

"At first, he was so kind and caring. I was excited to be the centre of his attention. And," she added, "he was good-looking and so good at swimmin' and most of the girls fancied 'im." Seeing his face change, she said quickly, "Don't get me wrong, Dom; I was foolish and I always liked you as well, but you were so shy and Rydd, well, he just took me over. Then he started kissin' me and tellin' me how special and pretty I was. He said I was the only girl for 'im. I believed 'im. But after that, he got jealous if I spoke to any other boy and then he got forceful that New Year's evenin'." She paused with embarrassment and the pain of the memory, "And, afterwards he pinned me against the wall and threatened me."

Dom flushed with anger. "He's such a bully, a real bad 'un." He felt not to tell her about all his suspicions; it might get her into trouble with Sid if he found out.

"From then on, I was scared of him; he's so strong and he controlled me more and more. I felt dirty and ashamed."

"There is nothin' for you to be ashamed of; it was not your fault. You are not just pretty, you're beautiful," Dom said. Their eyes met and she kissed him tenderly.

"Thank you so much for rescuing me that day. I'll never forget how brave you were! Like a knight in shining armour!"

He held her close.

"I'm scared now about havin' a baby, Dom. I'm so sorry."

He reassured her. "It was definitely not your fault. We'll make it through together and Prue will help you. Everything will be alright, you'll see." He sounded more confident than he felt.

But his optimism was soon to be shattered.

The first sign of trouble was when Jim Hoskin was unable to tend his bar at The Ship Inn.

"Whats'a matter with old Jimmy tonight then?" his mate, Tom Trelleck, asked Meg, as he downed his pint.

"E've got the runs real bad," she answered. "Came on after tea. Must be somethin' he ate – but," she suddenly realised the implication of her remark, "it ain't my cookin'!" she added, pointing her finger at Tom who grinned.

"Old Jimmy could always put it away," he said, knowingly.

But later that night it was clear he was really ill. Meg had changed the bedsheets twice and he was vomiting as well. His mouth was dry and when she gave him some water, he had only just swallowed it when he threw up again. Meg began to panic. "Lizzie," she called out to her daughter who was washing up the glasses at the back of the bar. "Yer dad's real poorly. I don't like the look of 'im. Run up to Dr Grey and make sure 'ee comes quick."

Lizzie, who was now a slim girl of thirteen, was scared by the tone of her mother's voice and sped up to the doctor's house like the wind. Mrs Grey answered her frantic knocking. "Me dad's real sick. Ma says can the doctor come right away?"

"I'm sorry, my dear. Doctor is out visiting a patient, but I'll send him as soon as he gets back."

When Lizzie returned, Meg was in a state. "Oh no what can we do? Yer dad looks real sick. 'is skin is a blue colour."

"I'll go 'elp him," offered Lizzie, moving to the stairs.

"No, don't," Meg said firmly. "It might be catchin'. Maybe he 'as a fever or flu but I ain't never seen 'im so bad as this. I'll see if he can take some drink."

She ran upstairs again with a bowl and a cup of water, only to find he had vomited again, all over the bedclothes. His face was pale and sweaty, and he couldn't speak; his eyes were closed.

"Jim, I've sent fer Doctor, ee'll be 'ere soon." But he never answered, nor did he seem to hear or be aware she was even there.

"O God," said Meg, "come on, Doctor, 'urry up!"

It was nearly midnight when Dr Grey arrived. She led him straight upstairs, telling him all about her husband.

He took his pulse and found Jim's heart was racing. He looked pale and wan and was sweating. "I don't like the look of this," he said grimly, noting the bluish tinge on his skin.

"It's strange, Doc, but his pooh is all milky and runny."

Dr Grey took some pills out of his bag and got them into Jim's open mouth and gave him some water. He swallowed them.

Within a few minutes he was sick again.

"Keep bathing his face and body to keep his temperature down," he ordered.

She looked blank at the big word he used. He realised and said, "It will keep the fever down."

"I need to go and check my medical book," he said. "I'll be right back. Oh, and keep your daughter away in case she catches it." He patted her arm and went out into the night. Meg was left wringing her hands. Lizzie appeared at the door, looking scared.

"You keep away. Doctor says it might well be catchin'. I think t'is best if you run down to Aunty Lil and ask 'er to keep you for the night."

"But Ma," whined Lizzie, "I don't want to. I'm scared fer dad. Why can't I 'elp you?"

But Meg's mind was made up. She insisted that Lizzie went right away.

It was just as well she did. At two in the morning, just before Dr Grey reappeared, Jim took his last breath and passed away. Meg screamed, "Jimmy, Jimmy come back. Don't leave me!" and she wept, sinking to the floor in her grief, while still holding on to his limp hand. "What am I goin' to do without 'ee? What'll become of me and Lizzy?"

At the thought of Lizzy losing her dad and never seeing him again, she wailed afresh.

Dr Grey, when he arrived, confirmed Jimmy's death. "I'm so sorry."

"Whatever will I do?" she wailed. "And what about Lizzie?"

He let her cry and then said gently, "Meg you need to drink plenty – it is very infectious – catching," he added.

"Why, what did 'ee 'ave?" she moaned.

"It was a serious fever," was all he would say. "You go and get some rest."

He walked out in a state of great concern.

The next morning, early, he called again. There was no answer. As no one in the village ever locked their doors, he entered and called out "Mrs Hoskin? Meg?" There was not a sound.

He went up to the bedroom and found her on the floor with her arm up, still gripping her husband's hand. She was lying in a pool of diarrhoea and vomit. She was dead.

He found a key behind the door and locked it. He went right out and called at the next-door neighbour's house. Annie Hiscock answered, and he told her the bad news. She fell back against the door in shock. He explained that it was a bad fever and please would she find Lizzie and break the news.

"But on no account let her go into the house. She must stay with her aunt. It is very catching. I will arrange for everything. Tell her there will be no school today."

He left in a hurry leaving her open-mouthed. He made his way directly back along Garrett Street and called at Pastor Kenny's house. Word of the tragedy sped around the villages like wildfire. Everyone repeated what Annie Hiscock had heard. "It's a very bad fever."

"Maybe it's the plague," said one. "'Tis certain strange that they both died so quick."

"Who'll run The Ship now?" An old fisherman asked.

"Poor Lizzie," said another, "both gone in one night! I guess her aunty'll look after her now."

But that day, another fell sick and Dr Grey was called again. Next time it was Rose Gill who lived on her own. No one knew she was sick till it was too late.

There was another case and another; all were in Garrett Street. All followed the same sort of pattern, with extreme diarrhoea and vomiting.

Fear gripped Cawsand. "It's a judgement," one mournful woman said to her neighbours, as they met in the street.

They agreed; "It's them deaths we 'ad; they've brought a curse on us."

"But whatever is the sickness?" Folk asked again and again.

Dr and Pastor Kenny had swiftly talked with Mr Trevelyan, who got the school closed to try to protect the children. Dr Grey had shared with Pastor Kenny after consulting his medical books.

"It is, I believe, cholera," he said in grave tones.

He quickly appraised the two men of the nature of the infection as he had learned from his medical tome. "The diarrhoea is grey, runny and milky; they vomit a great deal and become very thirsty and yet they cannot keep anything down. Their skin turns a bluish colour. There is a very rapid heart-beat and death comes very swiftly, in a matter of hours, unless they are kept hydrated."

"What treatment can we give to nurse them?" asked Pastor Kenny.

"I have sent a message to some doctor friends in Plymouth and Exeter for advice," he answered. "But just now I don't know. All we can do is try and keep them away from other people."

"And pray," added Pastor Kenny quietly. The three men decided to take action and use the school room as a sort of hospital, to try and nurse the sick and stop the infection spreading. Miss Jane offered to live with the Greys and help in the nursing.

That day, Lamorna stood anxiously at the wall overlooking the beach at the end of Garret Street. It was eight in the morning but she had sent a boy with a note and hoped Dom was there. She stood with her arms crossed over her shawl, looking out towards the Martyns' coastguard cottage. In a very few minutes she saw the figure of Dom in the garden and he waved. He had seen, even though the time was different. She hurried down the steep hill to the village square and avoided stopping until she had made it to the edge of Penlee woods, where Dom was waiting for her.

She told him all about the sickness and death in the village. He already knew, as Prue had heard it from her friends.

"What about Kingsand?" he asked.

"'Tis strange," she said, "but no one is sick over there, from what I've heard."

When she told Dom her dad was feeling a bit sick that morning, his mind was made up.

"Come and talk to Prue and Dad," he said, "you must come and live with us right away."

Ned was out. In conversation with Prue, who immediately grasped the situation, Lamorna was reluctant to leave her dad.

"How can I leave?" she asked. "What if he's gits this fever and he needs me?"

"You are not thinkin' straight," said Prue gently. "You have a baby on the way to consider. If you stay there, you and your baby could both die."

This did make sense to Lamorna and she nodded slowly. "But what about yer dad? Will he let me stay?"

Prue answered: "I've been talking' to 'im and he's comin' around. It'll be certain he will agree, especially when he hears about yer need and the fever in Cawsand."

"I'll go back and get some clothes and things," Lamorna said, getting up.

"Don't stay," warned Dom and Prue in unison.

Dom walked her back to the edge of the village and they agreed she would come as soon as she could.

He watched till she gave him a wave at the top end of Garrett Street, and she disappeared.

Back at her home, her dad was not in. The walk had made her thirsty, so she took a long cool drink of water. She wrote a note explaining that Prue had invited her to stay with a friend for a bit. She just felt unable to let him know the real reason. *Not yet,* she thought; *maybe later.* She gathered her clothes and some other things and took a few buns to give to Prue, along with some of her home-made jam. She had just popped them in a bag and was about to go when Jane Noakes, their next-door neighbour called in. She was full of the terrible deaths and believed it was a plague.

"Like the old days yers ago, the Black Death, they called it. What be us g'wain to do?" she asked frantically. As she talked on, Lamorna began to feel desperate. Suddenly, she was gripped with the need to relieve herself and so Jane left.

Midday passed. The day drew on. Still, in the afternoon light, Dom stood at the edge of the woods waiting, with his telescope scanning the houses and high wall above the beach for a sign of Lamorna; still, she didn't come. He began to fear she had got into an argument with her dad. Perhaps he had stopped her coming?

He felt desperate to find out so decided to slip into the village. When he got to her house, the door was ajar. He knocked but there was no answer. He felt a growing unease which made him decide to go in and check. There he found her on the floor of the kitchen, retching and groaning as she clutched her stomach.

"Dom," she gasped, "I feel terrible. No, don't come near. Get Doctor."

He raced out of the house in a panic but felt that he must ask Pastor Kenny to help him first, as the Manse was only a few yards away. Pastor Kenny immediately sprang into action saying, "We must get her up to the school room, where Dr Grey is working with all the sick. He'll know what to do." Outside, there was a horse and cart in the street. With a brief explanation the carter was willing to take them and they lifted Lamorna on to it. Dom was desperate to go with them, but Pastor refused very firmly.

"Dom, it's very infectious. I will take care of her, I promise. You'll help her best by keeping well. You need to go back. I will keep you in touch. I promise... Pray!" He called as the carter cracked his whip. Dom was left standing, helpless, with tears running down his face. Everything in him had wanted to stay with her but he felt convinced by the pastor's advice. He could trust her to him. He slowly turned and made his way home in an agony of mind.

Dr Grey had made contact with a medical friend of his in Exeter who had lived in India for some years. The reply to his letter informed him that this was a very serious disease. The letter included instructions on how to help the sick. It was very important to keep them hydrated with fluids, using regular small amounts of water with a spoon and to use opium for serious pain. The first few hours were vital.

Dr Grey wasted no time in informing Miss Jane. There were now ten patients in some distress. They had set up the school room as a make-shift hospital ward, with spare beds and pallets that had been loaned. The room was transformed; all the desks had been piled into an outdoor shed; the smell of carbolic soap filled the air. Dr Grey had succeeded in encouraging a nursing friend of Mrs Grey's to come over from

Plymouth to help them in this time of crisis. In addition to Miss Jane, Mrs Grey and Mrs Trevelyan were in attendance. Mrs Grey was a calm and efficient presence; she was used to dealing with sickness and had implicit trust in her husband. She was teaching Miss Jane how to fulfil their duties, especially the regular washing of their hands. Mrs Trevelyan was in a different state, full of fear. She was there out of a sense of duty and in obedience to her husband. Her angular face was flushed; her eyes fluttered constantly and she kept her handkerchief close to her mouth at all times.

Dr Grey was explaining: "From the symptoms I describe to him in my letter, my friend in Exeter, Dr Henson, recognises it as he has seen this disease in India. He says it is called cholera. The worst effect of the infection is that the body suffers from a lack of water due to the diarrhoea the infection causes. Although the patient cannot keep down normal drinking amounts, it is important to keep giving them two or three tablespoonfuls of water every quarter of an hour. We can also give them ten drops of laudanum for the pain. Castor oil can also be administered. If they last three days, apparently they may recover."

There was a noise and a flurry behind them. Mrs Trevelyan had fainted right away. They lifted her up on to a chair and Mrs Grey administered some smelling salts which brought her around.

"Oh dear, oh dearie me," she moaned. Mrs Grey comforted her, while Dr Grey prepared to continue.

"But how has this disease come about here?" interjected Miss Jane.

"He says it is often due to contaminated water. I have realised that all the patients are from the Cawsand side and none from Kingsand. Many are from Garrett Street. I suspect the village water from their pump has become infected."

"What about our water?" asked Miss Jane.

"As you will know, ours comes from a different pump in this village. It seems uninfected. We will, however, ensure everyone boils drinking water as a precaution."

At that moment, Pastor Kenny arrived with Lamorna.

"Oh, dear me," said the doctor. "Her father is already here and in very poor shape; now the daughter also." He pointed towards the corner, where Sid lay on a pallet, looking deathly pale and retching.

After Miss Jane called a lady to take care of her, the doctor resumed his suggestions for the treatment of the disease to her and Pastor Kenny.

"Infected water makes sense," said the pastor. "I had also realised it is mostly neighbours from my street. I have always boiled my drinking water, which is why, thanks be to God, I am not suffering. It must be the water from the pump. I must let everyone know to boil theirs to stop them from catching it."

"Dr Henson explains that it is contagious and can be passed by the mouth also," explained the doctor.

So saying, he moved away and began to inform all his helpers of the treatment they must give.

Pastor Kenny was as good as his word to Dom and spent much time in the schoolroom watching out for Lamorna, feeding her spoonfuls of water and praying for her, as he did for all the patients. He spread an atmosphere of calm with his steady service and was greatly appreciated by everyone there.

Meanwhile the numbers increased. On the next day, Connie Bolitho was brought in by her son Rydd who had carried her easily in his arms. He was eager to be gone from this sick place where everyone was weak and smelling of sweat.

"Besides," he muttered to the doctor, "me dad wants me fer some urgent business."

Dr Grey warned him to keep drinking but not to drink any water without boiling it. He went off in a mood.

"He's strong," the doctor said to Miss Jane. "He's a survivor. The fever probably won't get him."

Dom was in a fever of his own; a fever of fear and worry, as he waited for news; dreading it would be the worst. *Was he going to lose sweet Lamorna, after only so recently winning her?* He couldn't bear to think it. Prue did her best to give him hope and comfort. But in truth, however, she didn't think it looked good. Dom visited Pastor Kenny every evening for news, passing some people in the street who hurried past, holding scarves and handkerchiefs to their mouths. Fear stalked the streets like a tangible phantom. In the end, because of the spread of infection, Pastor Kenny sent a message to say he would come to Penlee woods every evening. The situation, he told Dom was very serious. He explained the often-fatal nature of the disease and the water connection.

"Will she live?" asked Dom desperately, horrified to hear the nature of the infection.

"We are doing our best for her. You need to pray."

Dom nodded. "Anything – only let her live," he sobbed.

Pastor told him about Lamorna's father already being there.

On the next day he said, "And there's someone else who has been brought in sick today who you know," he added.

"Who?"

"Connie Bolitho was brought in by her son Rydd, today."

"I hope he gets it. I hope he dies," cried Dom vehemently. "He's been nothin' but bad trouble; especially to Lamorna."

On one of their evenings at The Manse, he had shared everything about Lamorna to the pastor. Now his eyes caught Pastor's, looking intently at him.

"No matter what he's done," he said gently, "he needs our prayers too."

Dom couldn't agree. He went home praying hard to a God he wasn't even sure existed. He kept praying a single, simple sentence.

"Please God make her better," was all he kept praying. He was so obsessed with Lamorna's fate he never thought about the baby. He couldn't pray for Rydd. When he reached home Ned and Prue were both at home. Ned was working in the garden; Prue was in the kitchen. He burst in and broke the terrible news to Prue first; she immediately made plans to go and help nurse Lamorna. Dom was both pleased and afraid. "But Prue, you might catch it. I couldn't bear it if we lost you!"

"The poor girl needs someone who understands her other condition; no one else will know yet. I 'ave to go and help her; as and when I can. I know I must go, Dom, for her sake. She'll be frightened and besides," she added, "it is for you too."

Tears welled up in his eyes from an already over-full heart. He hugged her and whispered, "Thank you, Prue. But take care. Now I have two to pray for." At his words, Prue looked hard at him, with a question in her eyes at his use of the word 'pray'.

Prue went out to explain to Ned. Dom waited inside, wondering what he would say. She came back in, after quite a short time, to say, "Dad says he is sorry. He's letting me go as long as I come back and cook dinner each day."

Dom breathed a sigh of relief but was still fearful for Prue. He went out to thank Ned, who looked uncomfortable.

"Dad, thank you so much for letting Prue go." Dom said.

Ned turned away, "S'alright. I'm sorry for 'er," he muttered and went on digging.

It was as much as Dom could hope for. He went back to Prue who had gathered some things in a bag.

"I'm takin' some herbal treatments," she explained. Prue was always good at knowing about plants and remedies. She had learned a lot from Old Maudie, who was an expert. "There's pasties in the stove."

Dom hugged her tight and watched her go.

After a fairly silent meal of pasties, Dom had jobs to do for Ned involving planting seeds and chopping firewood and logs. As the afternoon was well on when he finished, he asked Ned if he could go out for a bit. Ned gave his permission.

"Keep yer eyes open if you be goin' near the sea and let me know of anythin' suspicious," he said, as he always did nowadays.

There was nothing else he could do. Dom knew where he was heading – the only place that gave him peace in troubled times.

Chapter 11
Rivals on Rame

"I looked upon the sea. It was to be my grave."[11]

It was a warm May evening. The sea was turquoise around the rocks, lapping lazily. Further out it was reflecting the coral pink clouds above. Over towards Rame the amber sun was low in the sky. The air was warm with a delicate breeze. It was so beautiful and tranquil, it made him catch his breath. *How could the world look so beautiful when such terrible disease was stalking the land, killing people a few miles from him?*

Dom made his way towards Rame, which reared up firm and steady before him. As always, he felt it reassure him somehow, as though it was telling him that it had always been there, immovable, and unchanging over the centuries. He approached the neck of land connecting it to the mainland and, as he did so, peace began to settle upon him to match the scene. He climbed to the top and settled himself where he could look out to sea. His thoughts were constantly returning to Lamorna.

---

[11] Mary Shelley

"O God, please make her better," he breathed. "Please, please, she's done nothing wrong. I love her!"

He ached with worry. *What if she was dying even as he spoke? What if they couldn't save her?* The thoughts came like wasps, thick and fast, stinging him. His panic grew and so did his praying. If only he had a picture of her! Her heart-shaped face and that gentle smile floated in his mind, like a balloon, as he went on speaking to the air.

He calmed down after some time. Over Looe and Polperro, the sun was setting in a glow of scarlet fire. He took out his telescope to scan the horizon and it was then that he spotted them. Right out just beyond the lighthouse was evidently some activity, involving several fishing boats. *They must have found a good shoal,* he thought. But, as he continued looking, it became evident that they were not fishing; they were lowering large stones into the sea attached by a rope. He adjusted the focus and homed in on them. There were several of the usual fishing boats but, as he moved slightly, he realised there was a big lugger with a French name on it. Figures were moving quickly and passing things from the lugger to the other boats. Working together, most had their backs to him. At that particular moment one of the larger men turned and Dom gasped. It was Bruiser! Next to him was the smaller shape of Richie's dad, Dick Grills. He realised this was smuggling business! He had heard of smugglers stowing contraband under the sea. They used special rocks, known as smugglers' stones as weights, with holes bored through them to tie the kegs of contraband with ropes. By using the weight of the stones, they could lower them in the deeper water. There they could lay hidden until hooking them up later at a safer time. Dom began to breathe fast. It must be, because of his dad's work for the Searchers and him living where he could easily see smuggling boats coming into Cawsand at night, Bruiser and his team had now resorted to this other way of keeping things hidden. They were obviously planning to use a different route.

He must alert Ned! He turned and ran, through the gathering dusk, back down the hill. Swiftly, over the neck of land and along the cliff path he pounded. At last, he rounded Penlee Point and swooped down through the woods to their home.

"Dad," he yelled, "Dad! Come quick!"

Ned appeared out from the house where he had been having some tea before setting off on his nightshift. Panting hard, Dom told him what he had seen.

For the first time, Ned said, "Well done!"

Dom flushed with pride. Ned, not noticing Dom's pleasure, sprang quickly into action and scribbled a note for Dom to run and get news to the nearest Searchers who lived on the hill over Maker way. While he wrote, Dom told his dad that he was pretty sure he had seen Bruiser and his team months earlier, landing goods below Rame. It was likely that some of the team would land there with some of the more easily distributed smaller goods and walk into the village under cover of the darkness, whilst the boats slipped back into the beach. Father and son parted ways. Ned borrowed Dom's telescope and headed for the coast towards Rame to see for himself. Dom set off over the hill on the shortest route.

As he ran over the hill in the warm summer evening, with the few lights of the wealthier homes twinkling in the villages below him, his heart was focused on the fate of Lamorna.

"O God," he found himself panting, "let her live, please let her live."

The words drummed in time to his pounding steps. He couldn't bear to think of losing her now that he had only just made her his own.

Dom breathlessly gave his message to Searcher Sam Lundy, who immediately said he would gather his mates, and at the same time, alert the Revenue boat from Cremyll. Dom walked back over the hill, catching his breath. He could not rest without knowing how Lamorna was. He made up his mind, whatever the news, he must know! He would call in at Kingsand school. Dim lights were evident in the windows from the candles inside as he walked in close darkness down the hill. His heart was beating fast in anticipation, mixing hope and fear. He knocked on the door. Mrs Grey answered and was surprised to see Dom there.

"Is there someone else ill?" she asked before he could speak.

"N-no," he stammered, "I want to know how Lamorna is."

"She's very poorly, Dominic," she answered sadly. "She can't see you."

"I must see her," his voice was anguished.

"You can't come in, Dominic. You might catch the cholera; it's very infectious."

"I must," his voice was louder.

Suddenly Pastor Kenny appeared behind Mrs Grey. "It's alright Mrs Grey, I'll handle it." She retreated gratefully.

"Dom," he said gently, "I'm so sorry. Prue is doing her best and is nursing her well, but she has had a setback and is very weak."

Pastor's words panicked him. "Please Pastor, please, I must see her. Let me at least see her."

Pastor Kenny, seeing his distress, relented. "You can come in Dom, for a quick look, but you mustn't get close to Lamorna or to anyone."

Dom felt a flood of relief. He followed the pastor into the dimly lit room. He caught his breath at the number of beds and the moans and groans coming from people. The stench of sickness was in the air. His eyes were searching and then he saw her in the far corner. Prue and Dr Grey were bending over the bed in which his loved one lay.

He advanced slowly and his movement caught Prue's attention. She stood up and came quickly over to him.

"Oh Dommy, you shouldn't have."

"I had to," his voice broke. "Prue, how is she? Will she live?"

"Dommy, we don't know but I am keeping close and doing everything I know how."

"Pastor said there was a setback – what is it?"

"Dommy, she has had a miscarriage and lost the baby. Doctor Grey is treating her."

"I must see her – please let me at least see her."

Prue took his hand and led him near enough. He could see Lamorna's face, shining with sweat. *White – oh so white!* Grey rings encircled her eyes. At that moment her eyes opened, and she saw him. Her mouth opened and broke into a weak smile. He smiled through his tears and raised his hand. Dr Grey was giving her small amounts of medicine.

"You must go now," came Pastor's deep voice behind him. "We don't want you catching it."

Dom turned and met his kind eyes. "Please, please pray for her, Pastor, please."

"Yes Dom, I am and I will. She is in God's hands. Prue is doing a good job. You keep praying too."

Dom nodded, and wiping his tears, he took a last look at Lamorna whose eyes were following him. He raised his hand to his mouth and blew a kiss. She smiled her wan smile. He stumbled out of the door.

As he paced slowly away into the darkness, his mind was reeling and his heart beating with emotion. The image of her sweet face, looking so drained of her natural colour; her weak smile, they danced before him; his thoughts raced. She had lost Rydd's baby! He had to admit, *that was a relief – but what if losing it had weakened her and might kill her?*

"O God!" He muttered again. "Let her live."

It took him a long time to get home as he was walking so slowly on the darkened rough paths. He almost didn't want to be walking away from Lamorna, increasing the distance between them. Several times he tripped over a tree root; there were strange noises in the woods and an owl was hooting eerily. It all added to his sombre and fearful mood.

At last, he saw the dim shape of the house ahead of him. As he expected, no one was at home. Wondering what was happening at Rame, he collapsed into a chair and exhausted with worry, he fell into a deep sleep.

Ned, after receiving Dom's message, had hurried, running and walking alternately, along the path to Penlee Point and then, along the wildly undulating path through the gorse towards Rame. The twilight had passed, and the sky was dark with only a faint pink smudge of sky over Looe's coastline to the west. After another twenty minutes he was crossing the bridge of land and began a careful ascent of the east side of Rame head. Once he slipped and landed on his bad shoulder with a sickening jarring of his arm. He nearly cried out in pain but stopped himself. As he gained the crest of the hill, he knelt on all fours and crawled to try and see if he could spot anything. It was the sounds that gave away the activity. He could hear cursing and angry words. There was the glint of lantern light every now and again. Clearly there was still much activity. He had to wait for Searcher Sam; there was nothing he could do on his own. He crawled closer and closer. The breeze off the sea refreshed him. Time passed.

At last, he was aware of scuffling steps climbing up behind him. He crawled back and whispered hoarsely.

"Sam – Sam?" He was answered by a whispered, "Ned, it's Sam. There's three of us."

The three men emerged like shadowy ghosts from the gloom. There was the glint of metal; each were armed with a pistol.

"The Revenue boat is coming," whispered Sam, "but you need to keep behind us and hold back; we haven't got a spare pistol."

Ned agreed as they made a swift plan. The three were going to advance and surprise the smugglers with a shot and a call to surrender.

They advanced over the brow of the hill and began to descend. There was still quite a bit of activity and swearing. Bad tempers were evident between Bruiser and his gang. He was cursing Richie and Sid for not being quick enough. This brought out Sid's mean streak and he apparently leapt on Richie, blaming him for being a weakling. At that point, as they could now see the men below them, Sam fired his pistol. The shot resounded dramatically in the night air.

"This is the Searchers," yelled Sam, and bluffing, he added, "there are more of us than you! So, stay where you are and give yourselves up! The Revenue boat is here."

Bruiser yelled wildly to his men, "Get down, damn you!" There was a flare of flame and he shot at the Searchers; there was a cry as someone was hit. Sam fired again. Bruiser and his men scattered down to their boats.

Dom was shocked awake by a hammering on the door. The dawn was breaking and the clouds were touched with fiery pink. On opening the door, he saw Sam Lundy, the Searcher, who had received his message. His lean, unshaven face looked serious, his breath was coming in short gasps.

"It's yer dad," he panted, "come quick!" His voice was urgent, his eyes gripping Dom's.

Dom shook himself wider awake. "Me dad? What's wrong?"

"He's bin hurt bad."

Dom jerked into action shutting the door behind him. "What's happened?"

Everything in Dom wanted to run wildly but Sam was out of breath from his run and was clearly struggling. As they hurried along, Sam began to fill him in with the story in breathless phrases. He told him how they met his dad and came upon Bruiser Bolitho's gang.

"There were at least six of them. We surprised the gang with a pistol shot but suddenly, another answerin' pistol shot rang out! We didn't know they had a gun! There was a scream – someone was wounded but in the dark we couldn't see who. Later, we saw it was yer dad."

Fear leapt up into Dom's throat. But Sam was continuing his story. He and his men began to duck behind rocks as they advanced. Some of the men were spotted and a fight broke out.

"Everythin' was confused in the darkness," Sam explained. "We were hitting wildly and falling over rocks. But then the Revenue boat arrived and their men trapped Bruiser's gang in a pincer movement between them and Sam's searchers higher up."

"But what about me dad?" pressed Dom anxiously.

Sam was slow of speech and not to be rushed. "Well, we were gainin' ground and pushin' them back to the sea. One younger one made off into the rollin' mist. The first one we caught was a runt, a skinny man, calls hisself Dick Grills – we tied him up along with the rest."

"Dick – that's Richie's dad," exclaimed Dom.

Sam continued: "Bruiser ran, firing his pistol back at us. But he ran right into the Revenue men from the boat. He put up quite a fight but they outnumbered him. They quickly overpowered him and tied him up."

"But what about me dad?" He was desperate to know.

"Well, it was after that we found yer dad. One of our men fell over 'im. He was lyin' between the rocks."

"Yes, but is he alive or dead?" Dom was exasperated with Sam and was now in a fever of anxiety.

They had rounded Penlee Point and the head protruding out into the sea was clearly visible rising above the pink morning mist. The neck of land joining it to the mainland was hidden and so Rame looked like a disembodied island.

"He was alive when I left 'im but he'd lost a lot of blood from a wound in his neck. He wouldn't let us move 'im; said we must get you quick." The boat had sailed off taking Bruiser and the rest of his gang. "We left our youngest to guard him and try to keep him warm."

Now that Sam had regained his breath, they both began to run. But the bad news added wings to Dom's feet and he raced ahead. His eyes were focused on Rame where his dad was injured.

"Oh God, keep him alive, keep him alive," he muttered as he ran.

The sea was growing pink as the sun rose over Plymouth way, dispersing the mist. It would have been beautiful if Dom had not been faced with potential tragedy.

He leapt up on to the neck of land and began to scramble up the steep hillside.

"Where is he?" he yelled back to Sam.

"Keep going to the left to t'other side," came Sam's shout from a hundred yards behind.

Rounding the steep side, Dom was facing the sea, but his eyes were searching the rocky slope.

Suddenly, he saw a man kneeling over a body just fifty yards below.

Dom bounded down over the rocks like a goat, nearly twisting his ankle several times. He never felt the pain. All that mattered was to get to his dad.

When he reached him, he was shocked. Ned was covered with an old coat; his eyes were closed; his skin was like white parchment and the rag the man was holding against his neck was dyed totally scarlet with Ned's blood.

"Is he dead?" he cried. "Dad! Dad!"

Ned's eyes opened. Dom was shocked to see how dark they were – it seemed he had never been close enough to notice before. Dom laid one hand on his dad's head and with the other he grasped the cold and clammy hand.

Ned's mouth grimaced with pain – his lips began to move. "Dom," he panted, "Dom, you've come!"

"Yes, Dad I'm here." Dom's voice broke.

"Dom, I'm dyin'."

"No dad," Dom's voice was desperate. "We'll get you 'ome – get Dr Grey."

Ned shook his head, "No Dom, it's too late."

The tears began to fill Dom's eyes and dripped on to Ned's gaunt face.

"Listen Dom… I want to say I'm sorry fer the way I've treated you… I wanted to love you but some'ow I couldn't."

"It's alright Dad, don't worry."

Ned shook his head. "No, Dom, it's not alright. I've bin a hard man. Please" – he paused and gathered more breath – "I want you to forgive me. I was wrong to blame you for yer ma's death; It wasn't your fault. I'm sorry son. Yer a good lad. I'm sorry. Forgive me?" Ned's voice was raised in the last question and his eyes searched Dom's.

Dom's eyes overflowed. "Dad I forgive you; I forgive you." He hugged his dad and, as he did so, felt something hard break and give way in his heart. Ned's hand gripped his hand hard.

Then Ned smiled and, with his last breath, he was gone.

Dom cried for a long time, his head on his father's chest. When he raised it, the smile was still on his father's face.

At that moment, men arrived with a rough stretcher to carry Ned, as they thought, to a doctor. Realising he was dead; they expressed their sympathy in simple words.

"We was asked to take him to Dr Grey and Mr Trevelyan's," they said.

"No," said Dom, firmly, "it's too late for the doctor. Take him to Pastor Kenny. He may be at the school if he's not at the Manse in Garrett Street."

They left him sitting stunned on the cliffside, facing the rising sun over a rosy sea. It was a beautiful morning. His thoughts and emotions were conflicted. He sat there a long time thinking about his dad and their reconciliation; his eyes filled again. It was too late, yet it brought him comfort. *Poor Prue,* he thought, *we're orphans now.* Finally, his thoughts returned again to Lamorna.

"O God," he said again, "let her live – please let her live." His prayer for his Dad hadn't been answered. *Would this prayer be?*

He rose. He must get back to her.

He climbed back up to the chapel at the top. He went into its empty shell.

"God, if you're real, as Pastor Kenny thinks, please let Lamorna live." It struck him that he was making a lot of prayers lately – but were they being answered? A strange sense of peace stole over him; he was surprised. He gazed out of the window towards Penlee Point. Behind it, in the old school room where they had been taught, she was lying there.

He stirred himself and began the descent down the steep back of the headland towards the bridging neck of land. But he never got across it.

Without warning, from a large rock behind him, a body hurled itself at him, knocking him to the ground.

He turned to see Rydd's wild face contorted with anger. Rydd's fist hit his face, momentarily stunning him. He rolled away and staggered to his feet.

"You bloody traitor, bloody dumb Dommy," Rydd spat the words out; his eyes glittering with evil. "You and yer cowardly dad!"

His words sung Dom into action. "My dad's dead because of you and your kind," he yelled and he felt the anger rise up in him.

They circled each other like prowling wolves. Rydd's black mane of hair was blowing wild in the wind; his eyes were dark and gleaming with murderous hatred. His mouth was curling in contempt. He lunged and they locked in combat. Dom felt the force of Rydd's weight pressed against him and lost his balance. They rolled together in a wrestling grip down the path onto the narrowest part of the bridge of land. Dom freed an arm and had a chance to give a good punch into Rydd's belly. It winded him, giving Dom chance to stand up. In a trice, Rydd was on his feet in fury. He swung a right towards Dom's jaw, but Dom moved his face sideways to avoid it.

"You're finished," spat Rydd. "You took my woman and I'm going to take you out, you turd!"

"Lamorna is mine now – you'll never have her," panted Dom, putting up his guard, as Tris had taught him.

"She's carryin' my kid – she's mine." He dodged sideways and smashed his fist behind Dom's guard, straight into his eye.

Dom yelled in pain; his eye was on fire.

Rydd took advantage of the moment and came at Dom with full force, hitting him like a battering ram and pushing him back to the edge of the cliff. Dom looked down and saw the jagged line of rocks seventy feet below, rising up out of the deceptively beautiful turquoise waters swirling with foam around them; they were like jaws of teeth ready to devour him.

They locked again. "No," shouted Dom, his eye closing up, "she's not carryin' your baby – its died!"

Rydd, jerked back in astonishment. "You're lyin'," he snarled.

"No, I visited," panted Dom. "Prue told me, she's lost it!"

Rydd gave a primeval scream. He leapt upon Dom like a black panther. His agility caught Dom by surprise. The force of his lunging attack knocked them both backwards. Rydd's hands were grasping for his neck and they fell off the bridge path towards the waters below, locked as one, like murderous lovers. As the air rushed by him, with Rydd's face snarling in his, Dom waited for the terrible impact of the rocks which would surely cut them in half. This was the end.

Instead of the rocks, they landed with a bone-jarring blow on a narrow ledge of grassy cliff just above the water. The impact winded Dom, who was now trapped underneath Rydd's heavy body. Before he could move out from under his antagonist, Rydd was on his knees. Grabbing Dom's arm, he forced it up his back so that he was able to push him over the edge. Dom felt the power of Rydd's other muscled arm around his chest, his hot breath on his neck; the hateful words were still flowing from Rydd's snarling mouth.

"Die, damn you, die!"

With that, he forced Dom over the edge but Dom's other arm gripped Rydd's thigh and again, they plummeted as one, down into the waters. All Dom could see was deep green waters racing towards him, with Rydd on his back. Rydd's grip was unrelenting.

They narrowly missed the razor-sharp rocks. As the green waters covered his head and bubbles swirled around him, Rydd's strength was pushing him ever deeper, in a vice-like iron grip. Dom suddenly realised in a flash of revelation: this was his dream – his oft-repeated nightmare! It was happening now! He was drowning! The revelation shocked him and he momentarily lost his focus. Rydd's powerful hands moved to tighten in a deadly stranglehold around his neck; he squeezed and squeezed. Rydd's arm was still tightly encircling his chest like a giant snake. With that and the pincer grip around his neck, he could no longer breathe. The air already in his lungs was being forced out of Dom's body; his chest was heaving and his lungs felt as if they were bursting. Lamorna's lovely heart-shaped face rose before him. *He must fight for her!* He writhed and struggled with all his strength; trying with his hands to free his neck from the constricting hand-lock; if only he could get Rydd's weight off his back! But he was weakening; his life breath was bubbling past his face. He felt the desperate panic of so many times before. His mouth opened, longing to breathe. As he lost consciousness, he was fleetingly aware that something had changed; the weight was being peeled off his back; the hands gripping him were being loosed. But darkness swallowed him.

He was choking, lying on his side. Water was pouring from his throat. There was a warm orange light beyond his eyelids. He choked again; more seawater gushed from him; his lungs straining. He opened his eyes to see Sol's worried face looming in front of his.

"Dom, Dom," he cried, "Dom come back; don't die!"

He gulped air into his tortured lungs; he couldn't get enough. He felt terrible – but he was not dead. The dream was vanquished. He was looking at dear old Sol who was kneeling astride him. The worry and fear on his face faded and Sol's big mouth broke into a smile.

Remembering the fight, Dom jerked awake. "Where's Rydd?"

"Ee's gone, Dom: he's finished."

"What do you mean?" He raised himself up on one arm and saw they were lying on the sandy beach.

"I got 'im off you – I pulled 'im off. Then he was taken by a wave. I dragged you up and brought you in."

"Sol, where is he now?" Dom couldn't shake off the dread that any moment Rydd would appear and attack again.

"The wave took him and he got caught in the current – it's goin' out. It dragged 'im out. I see'd 'im; his arms were raised up and then he disappeared under the water. I never see'd him again."

Dom realised it was the treacherous undertow of Whitsands bay on the outgoing tide that had claimed many a life.

"But," he gasped, "you, Sol. What are you doin' here? What made you come?"

"It was Ma. Late last night Ma told me she had a feelin' you were in danger and she saw you drownin' off Rame head. She told me to run. I runned through the night and was searchin' fer you. From a ways back I saw'd you fightin' on the rock bridge and then you both fell. I came runnin' and climbed down. I see'd you both fall of the ledge with Rydd on your back. I ran down and dived in."

"Sol." Dom grabbed his sodden arm and pulled him close in gratitude. "Sol, you've saved my life. I'll never forget this – or you."

Sol began to shake and cry and hugged Dom harder than he'd ever been hugged before. And so, they lay on the sand as the sun rose higher over Rame and the gulls screamed and wheeled around them.

Chapter 12
A Restoration and a Resolution

"Heaven is boundless, and the sea is beneath you." [12]

The wedding ring clattered on to the chapel floor. There was a gasp from the congregation. Sol flushed bright red and, in confusion, scrabbled on the floor. He picked it up, giving it back to Dom, with shaking hands. His face was beaded with sweat. "Sorry Dom, sorry."

"It's okay, Sol, it's okay." Dom smiled at his bride and patted Sol's shoulder. Pastor Kenny was also smiling reassuringly.

Today the small chapel was full, to standing room only, with people from both villages; many of whom had never put a foot in the place nor ever expected to do so. They didn't know the chosen hymns, but their red faces were beaming on this occasion of happiness and hope after the dark days of cholera. Pastor Kenny was now a hero to them all. He had risked his life daily when he had no need to do so. He had helped to comfort and pray for all; for many of the victims he had been there to give them their last rites and prayers, often

---

[12] Rich Shapero

holding their hands, when no other relatives could be permitted near, due to the contagious nature of the disease. The epidemic had shaken the communities as never before.

It had also shaped them. The age-old rivalry had been overcome by shock at the many deaths and by shared sorrow, and compassion for the suffering of all those from Cawsand's Garrett Street. Once the epidemic was over, and even before it, many parcels of food, vegetables and fruit were donated from Kingsand as well as from other folk in Cawsand beyond Garrett Street. The Pascoes had really stretched themselves and given much of the produce regularly from their store. There were many absent today who were its victims. The saddest was Dr Grey, another hero of the community, who had succumbed to the disease towards the end of his valiant efforts. He had given himself unstintingly with hardly any rest and it was thought he had become so weak that his body was too vulnerable to resist the contagion. He followed his wife, who had nursed at his side and passed away a week earlier. Mrs Trevelyan had remained full of fear and had been persuaded, much to her relief, to withdraw from the little ward but too late; she had succumbed. Connie Bolitho, Sid Stephens, Jim and Meg Hoskins and others: twenty in all, had lost their lives and died apart from their family. No family member had even been able to see their loved ones to say goodbye, or to give them comfort. After the 'plague' was finished, the mourning was not. A heavy, almost tangible, atmosphere of grief pervaded the village for weeks. At the shops, in the Square, and especially around Garrett Street there could be seen regular meetings of neighbours, weeping as they tried to comfort one another in their many losses.

All of those tending the sick so sacrificially were now regarded as heroic and accorded much praise and whatever gifts of food that could be found. Dr Grey and his wife's memory was marked with a special service in Mr Trevelyan's chapel. Prue and Dom had attended it, remembering the doctor's acts of kindness and generosity to their family. Pastor Kenny was invited to lead it and speak, which went to show how much had changed since the epidemic. He, particularly, as one who wasn't medical, was respected by all for his sacrifice, standing in their place with the sick. Along with Mr Trevelyan and other local vicars, he had taken on a share of the many funerals, bringing consolation to many. Miss Jane and Prue were also held in high esteem for their service in those painful and trying weeks. Prue never again experienced any resentment in shopping at, or passing through, Cawsand. She, having mourned their dad for some weeks, was now ready to welcome the new bride and groom to share their house. Their continued tenure of the house was happily made possible because Dom's help and courage along with the loss of his father, had moved the Searchers, especially Sam, to recommend him as a coastguard in training. His telescope was also going to be a vital, extra help!

Dom never ever thought he would reach this day, his sixteenth birthday, let alone for it to be his wedding with the lovely Lamorna at his side. When she had entered the chapel on the arm of her uncle, he thought his heart would burst; she looked so lovely but natural. She wore a simple white dress and had flowers in her hair. She looked down the aisle to reassure herself and found his face turned towards her with his mouth open in wonder. It made her smile and took away her nerves. As the vows were repeated, word by word after

Pastor Kenny, who was smiling throughout the ceremony, he marvelled again and again at his beautiful bride.

"Now, Dom, you may kiss your bride," boomed Pastor Kenny's joyful voice. The chapel erupted in cheers and clapping, as Dom gladly obeyed. Some of the regular chapel members were a bit shaken by the noise and exuberance; this wild emotion was not their usual worship experience!

Looking at her happy, heart-shaped face, framed under the flowers in her hair, his eyes filled with tears. The news that she had survived, and nursed back to health by Prue, had been the best day of his life, until now. When Prue came home that momentous day, he was waiting with baited breath, filled with anxiety; as on every day for the last seven days. He had received verbal news from Prue each day but had not been given permission to visit again because of the increasing infection.

On this particular day, she had hurried through the door with a beaming smile on her face and said, "She is comin' home in a day or two, Dommy."

He fell into her arms and sobbed. Then, to her surprise, he fell on his knees and said, "Thank you God," over and over again.

The dreaded weight was lifted from his heart in those few seconds. Two days later he went to collect her. She was waiting, seated on a chair by the door. As she stood, holding on to the chair, he gasped at her weakness and frailty. The pallor and shrunken cheeks of her face told the story of her suffering. He hurried to gently embrace, and support her, kissing her, even though Pastor Kenny and Miss Jane were standing there. Pastor had arranged a cart and horse to convey her to her new home with Dom and Prue.

In the wedding service, just behind Lamorna, stood her bridesmaid, Lizzie Hoskins. She was smiling and crying at the same time, the bridal bunch of flowers shaking in her hand. She and Lamorna were now both orphans and had comforted each other, once Lamorna had recovered, as they were always close neighbours and friends. She stood proudly by Prue's side. Prue was matron of honour; both of them in pink dresses with bonnets decorated with late roses. Old Maudie was there, resplendent in a new shawl, over a best dress loaned to her, and her hair combed, watching her Sol being best man with swelling pride.

On the exact same day, miles away in Bodmin jail, Bruiser Bolitho was led out of the dirty, dark and dank cell where he had languished for months in total isolation. He had been sleeping on a plank 'bed' with no coverings and subsisting on meagre bread and gruel. The man who had been the big boss, controlling everyone; who had sailed the ocean in freedom wherever and whenever he chose, was left powerless in a small filthy cell to await his fate as a mere nobody, the lowest of the low; hated and all alone. The jail had been built by prisoners of war in 1779 and its purpose was revenge not reform.

Chained and dragged along by two jailers, Bruiser could not have looked anything less like the bully he had always been. His frame was still big but he had drastically lost weight on his deprived subsistence diet. His hair and beard were long, unkempt and greasy. He had been kept in total isolation. His face bore marks of being recently punched; his clothes were torn and filthy. Bully Bill 'Bruiser' Bolitho was cowed without his henchmen and out of his depth. Brought before a packed courtroom, he was tried for his offences. Judge

Jameson, summing up the case, declared with great gravity, "William Bolitho, you are found guilty on two counts. One, engaging in smuggling activity, transporting contraband in contravention of our sovereign King George the fourth, and the laws of this land, for which the penalty would have been transportation to the colonies. However," in a dramatic pause, he placed a black cap on his bewigged head. There were audible gasps from the courtroom. The judge continued, "On count two, you are judged guilty of the murder of one Ned Martyn, a Penlee coastguard at Rame Head in the region of the Edgecumbe estate in East Cornwall, on the night of 15th May this year of our Lord 1821. On the evidence of the witness of the Revenue man, one Samuel Lundy, you murdered him in cold blood, by the shot of a pistol in the course of smuggling contraband. The penalty for murder is execution. Therefore, the sentence of this court is that you will be taken from this court and hanged by the neck until you are dead."

At these words, a murmur of satisfaction ran like a wave across the court. Bruiser sagged in the dock and his chains rattled as he covered his face with his hands. The jailer yanked him away and out through the door. At noon that day Bruiser was taken by cart, held firmly by his two jailers, accompanied by a clergyman, out to the public gallows. Huge crowds surrounded him, spitting and jeering; some were throwing rotten tomatoes and eggs. The women of Bodmin, particularly, had developed a taste for hangings and gathered early to get the best view. This was their day out and their gruesome entertainment. At the gallows, the masked executioner was waiting. It was at this point that Bruiser's composure completely cracked and, in a panic, he began to dig in his heels and wrestle with his jailers, screaming aloud in his rough voice. For once, Bruiser, the supreme fixer and dodger of all entrapments, could not get his own way in his final extremity. The jailers were two beefy men who were used to this sort of scene. One of them gave him a sharp crack on the head with his truncheon. Dazed and bleeding, he was led to the gallows, where the rope was placed around his neck. The Clergyman recited a prayer for God's forgiveness and mercy upon him and stepped back. As the trap door opened with a loud crack, releasing him to the long drop, the jeering crowd, having watched avidly and having been pent-up with suspense and anticipation, gave blood-curdling screams of delight; cheering rent the air and hats were thrown up in great joy. Bruiser Bolitho left the world quicker than he had entered it. No one mourned his passing.

Unaware of this momentous event, the wedding party emerged with joy from the little chapel, crowding the little lane a few yards off Garrett Street. Outside the chapel door, Lamorna sought out Sol, who was standing at the back of the crowd.

"Sol, I can never thank 'ee enough; you saved my Dom's life. Without you this wedding would never have 'appened. You are always welcome at our 'ouse." Sol grinned and stood wringing his hands and stammering, not knowing what to say.

But when Lamorna reached over and kissed him on the cheek, tears filled his eyes; he blushed bright red. He had never been kissed by a girl before! It made his day!

As flower petals were thrown over the couple amidst much laughter and clapping, various comments could be heard from the crowd.

"They be so young."

"… Ah but they've been through 'ell… bless their 'earts; they both lost family, didn't they…? Now they have each other… love conquers all!"

Dom turned to find Pastor Kenny at the back of the crowd. "Pastor, I can never thank 'ee enough."

"It's a joy, my son," beamed the pastor. "This is a very joyful day. I am so proud of you."

"Pastor, can I come and see you sometimes? I think I will need your help to be a good husband."

"Certainly, my boy, it will be a privilege and pleasure. Now, off you go and enjoy your bride!"

Dom impulsively leaned forward and hugged him. He turned to re-join Lamorna and didn't see the tear in the pastor's eye.

He lifted Lamorna up on to the cart which the pastor had hired. Together they laughed with happiness as some of the crowd of well-wishers and children followed. Cheers echoed through the street, creating a new atmosphere in Garrett Street. Dom was full of pride as he held the reins and took the road down the steep hill through Cawsand with his 'Morna' holding his arm. People in the Square gave cheery waves and smiles at the newly married couple. Dom led the cart up the hill on the road towards Whitsands.

Lamorna looked surprised.

"Dom, where are we heading?"

"Ah," he smiled, "as we can't afford a honeymoon, I am taking you to share my special place."

In a short while they turned off and passed the old St Germanus church and on around the winding bends until they emerged at the top of the hill. Lamorna gasped at the beauty of the scene that lay before them.

Rame's headland was beset below them, surrounded on all sides by the vast blue sea in the autumnal sunshine. Hand in hand, Lamorna in her bridal dress and Dom in his smart suit, descended the hill, past the wild ponies, until they reached the narrow bridge of land. The memories of his near-death experience were swept away and replaced by the long kiss they enjoyed as he led her carefully over. Together, they climbed the hill; at the little chapel, Dom kissed her again. They went outside to face the distant horizon.

"Oh, how beautiful it is!" exclaimed Lamorna, with her arms around him.

Never again, would he experience the nightmare dream: it was vanquished.

"Yes," he replied, "it was my special place but now it's ours."

The End